REGARDING KIMBERLEY

Vera Berry Burrows

Regarding Kimberley

"I'm home," Ben called when he arrived in from work. The house was silent. "That's odd," he said out loud. "Belinda?" Still there was no response. He went into the kitchen where he found his wife sitting at the breakfast bar, her head in her hands. "Bel? What's the matter?"

Belinda lifted a tear-stained face and looked at Ben with sheer desperation in her eyes. "She's fallen in love with an Australian," she said quietly.

Ben sighed audibly. "I assume you're talking about Kimberley," he said.

"A bloody Australian!" Belinda said more loudly.

"Well, what's so wrong with that, babe?" Ben asked.

"She can't go to live in Australia. The risks would be too great. It will be the end of our family. She'll..."

"Calm down for goodness sake, Bel," Ben coaxed.

"She must be mad," she snapped. "And I told her so. We've had a row like never before. She more or less told me that my opinion means nothing to her. She isn't going to tell me what she's doing, or where she's going ever again."

"That's just Kim, isn't it? You know she doesn't like being told what to do."

"That's an understatement if ever there was one," Belinda rejoined. "Think about it, Ben. It's the same situation Joel had with *his* mother. God forbid she should take the same road through life as he did."

"Look, Bel, you can't blame Joel every time Kim does something you don't like. You know as well as I do that he has had absolutely no influence on her life..."

"She has his genes and that's enough for me," Belinda interrupted.

"I can't deny that and you take every opportunity to rub in the fact that he's her father and I'm not. I've done everything in my power to raise Kim as my daughter. I love her and I respect the person she has become, but I don't need you reminding me constantly that I had nothing to do with her conception." Ben was becoming angry and Belinda started to cry again. "And don't use your tears to soften me up. I'm over it, Bel. I suggest you get over it too, or it will be the end of us and it will be your fault, not Kim's and not Joel's. Enough is enough!"

REGARDING KIMBERLEY

Vera Berry Burrows

A Wings ePress, Inc.
Mainstream Novel

Wings ePress, Inc.

Edited by: Jeanne Smith
Copy Edited by: Joan Powell
Senior Editor: Jeanne Smith
Executive Editor: Marilyn Kapp
Cover Artist: Trisha FitzGerald

All rights reserved

Wings ePress Books
http://www.wings-press.com

Copyright © 2010 by Vera Berry Burrows
ISBN 978-1-61309-944-5

Published In the United States Of America

Wings ePress Inc.
3000 N. Rock Road
Newton, KS 67114

Dedication

To my husband, Alan Burrows whose mastery of the English language is more useful to me than the Oxford Dictionary and to my dear friend, Carole Cullen who is the most wonderful inspiration to me at all times.

One

August 1995

"Shock doesn't come anywhere near to how I feel." Her voice was weak and trembling. "I spent almost thirty years thinking I had the perfect family. I had a mother who cared for me and was my best friend, a dad who was the best in the world, a brother who was the proverbial pain in the backside, but was always there for me," she explained. "In the past half hour, my world has been completely smashed to smithereens."

"I don't know what to say, babe," Simon told her. "I can't imagine what is going on inside your head, but I want you to know I love you. I'm here for you and whatever you decide to do, I'll support you every step of the way."

Kim looked directly into Simon's eyes. "Do I really look like Joel Winston?" she asked.

Simon smiled affectionately. "Yes, I'm afraid you do."

~ * ~.

1986

Belinda Mason was distraught. "Why on earth did you have to bring all that up after all this time?" she asked her husband.

"I didn't deliberately bring it up, Bel. I just wondered if she'd discussed the job with you and said you knew more than I did about the world of entertainment. Sorry, babe. She didn't pursue the topic, so I don't think you have anything to worry about. Anyway, what harm would it do for you to give her a little helpful, motherly advice?" Ben reassured her. "The past we've kept hidden for so many years really is safe. You have to believe that."

"You know Kimberley, Ben. Simple answers never satisfy her. She has to know every minute detail before she'll let it rest. She's like a dog with a bone. She's self-assured and very insistent..." then thinking, *I'd like to say 'just like her father,' but that would be cruel and uncalled for.* "Let's just hope she is too preoccupied with the preparation for her interview to think about me."

"I think you're worrying unnecessarily," he said gently. "She'll have too much on her mind to dwell on it. Just think about it, Bel. In all these years, she has never once brought up that trip to Australia and for an eight year old, it was quite something at that time. I can't begin to understand why she has chosen never to talk about it, knowing how inquisitive she can be."

"That's probably because you and I agreed, rightly or wrongly, not to talk about it when we arrived home and she was too busy catching up on the school work she missed, not to mention her piano lessons. Don't forget it was Christmas time and Santa had left her presents here for when she came home. As regards the other situation, I know we made our peace with Joel, but what happened is always going to be an unpleasant memory for me. I really don't like to think about it, never mind talk about it and certainly not to our daughter."

Ben knew Belinda would never totally get over the part of her past that changed her life in ways she could never have imagined. She had built a protective wall around herself to cut herself off from that bit of her life. He took his wife in his arms. "I love you, Belinda Mason."

"I love you too," Belinda told him and that was all Ben needed to hear.

~ * ~.

After she left university with a first-class honours degree in business studies, Kimberley Mason's part-time job at the Bolton Royal Theatre presented her with an opportunity too good to miss. An ageing entrepreneur, Theodore Pendennis, who came from Liverpool took over the theatre. "I would like to inject some life into this old building," he said with an authoritative air. "I intend to give this theatre back to the people. From what I have seen, there is a lot of excellent talent in this town. We need to be able to present it to the public in a theatre that looks the part."

Pendennis, Kim learned, had a long theatrical history. She had never heard of him before he turned up in Bolton, but she felt inspired by his manner that oozed style and confidence. His military bearing was impressive and his upright stance gave him an air of superiority. Kim smiled to herself. The twenty-one year old Miss Mason was stage-struck. *I'm totally in awe of this man, even though he is a bit aloof,* she thought as she listened to his plans.

"I shall post a list of situations vacant within the next few days," Pendennis announced to the assembled theatre staff. "Some will be quite menial tasks, but nonetheless important to the smooth running of the theatre. Others will require academic qualifications and will be advertised in the local press as well as in *The Stage* magazine. Interviews will take place next month." His no frills manner left the few part-time theatre workers under no illusions. "If you want a particular job, you'll have to prove your worth."

When the list appeared, Kim couldn't contain her excitement. "Look at this, Dad!" she called out as soon as her father arrived home from work at the bank. Waving the job specifications in his direction, she said, "It's perfect! I couldn't wish for a better opportunity. Finding a decent job has been hard since I left uni. Being a ticket seller and usherette in a broken-down theatre has hardly been worth getting a degree for, but look at this…"

Ben Mason put down his briefcase, removed his coat and exchanged it for the piece of paper that Kimberley was offering him. "Hang my coat up for me, sweetheart, and let me see what all the fuss is about." He sat in the lounge of their Harwood home, the place he and Belinda had bought when Joel Winston and his mother left to start a new life in Australia. Momentarily, he thought of Joel. *Don't hear from him these days. Out of sight, out of mind, I suppose. Funny I should think of him now. Maybe it's this list of jobs in the theatre.* "Is this what you're interested in—theatre cleaners?" he asked as he scanned the list of vacancies.

"Dad, don't be facetious," Kim chastised.

Ben scanned the list again: "Stage Manager, Musical Director, Production Assistants, Stage Crew, Make–up Artists, Costume Designers, Wardrobe Mistress …Are you sure you're qualified for these jobs, Kim?"

Kim was becoming irritated. "I'm not qualified for the theatrical jobs; of course, I'm not," she said pointedly, "but look at the bottom of the list: Personal Assistant to Theatrical Agent—must have business acumen."

"Have you talked to your mum about this? She knows a little bit about working in the entertainment industry."

"Mum does? How come? I never knew Mum was an old pro," Kim said, a bemused expression on her face.

"Kimberley Mason!" her dad exclaimed. "Wash your mouth out with soap and water! An old pro? Whatever do you mean?" he said laughing at the thought. "Where is she anyway?"

"She's taken Tony to his soccer training. Why that boy can't go on the bus, I don't know. It's about time he learned to drive, then

Mum wouldn't have to mollycoddle him. Anyway, tell me about Mum's stage career. Was she an actress, a dancer, a singer? I can't believe she never talks about it. It's even more exciting if I'll be following in Mum's footsteps."

"It isn't important to her anymore. Nothing ever came of it because she was expecting you at the time. She used to sing a bit, but she wanted to be a make-up artist, or a set designer, then you came along and that was that." He stopped abruptly and wondered if he had disclosed too much.

"It would have been more exciting than being a hairdresser," Kim said, "but then being a hairdresser is similar to being a make-up artist, I suppose. Second best, though."

"She's a beautician and, like I said, the past is not important. Anyway, if you're going to apply for this position, you'd better work on your interview skills. Would you like me to put you through your paces?" he continued, thinking, *I really ought to steer her away from Belinda's past.*

"No thanks, Dad. I have to be confident enough to do this on my own and apart from that, you know I don't like you telling me what I should do."

Ben nodded knowingly.

"My business degree covered everything necessary," she continued. "Now it will be a case of whether or not I am able to put my knowledge into practice. I can't wait."

Ben regarded the daughter he loved with all his heart and soul. "Top marks for enthusiasm, Princess. Good luck, or should I say break a leg?"

Kim giggled. "I never did understand the implications of that remark, but I'd turn up on crutches for my interview if I had to."

"I think it's a bit of reverse psychology," Ben told her. He watched as she took the list of jobs and turned to leave the room. "Mind your step," he quipped.

"Very funny, Dad," Kim said with a withering look. "You just watch this space."

Two

When Kimberley got the personal assistant's job, it was just before her twenty second birthday. The Premier Plus Agency was run by Robert De Montford, the protégé of Theodore Pendennis who owned the London organization. She found out Pendennis had left Liverpool when Maria Morenzi passed away. "Who are all these people?" she asked Robert as they relocated to the temporary Manchester office.

"Well…" Robert said with a theatrical pause, "Maria Morenzi was a dancer from Liverpool who opened a theatre school down by the docks, at first for under-privileged kids. It became one of the most famous schools in the country and she traded on her experience of being in the Folies Bergere in Paris and a Windmill Girl in London during the nineteen thirties. Theo told me she was very close to Maurice Chevalier."

"Who?"

"Oh, you young people!" Robert exclaimed, throwing his arms in the air. "Don't you know anything about the wonderful stars of the stage and screen? You've never lived." He stood hand on hips as he continued. "However, for your information, Maurice Chevalier was a French star, considered to be the sexiest man on earth in his day. Not my type, you know," he said with a wink in Kim's direction, "but Theo told me Maria was very close to him, to Maurice I mean, and to Arthur Askey."

"Who?"

Robert gave her a disparaging look. "Shush, Kim and listen. You might need all this background information when you're looking for up and coming talent. You would do well to research the history of the theatre from Vaudeville to the present day, just for finding out how entertainment has evolved. Some of the older generation still like to wander down memory lane and the tribute bands that seem to be appearing just now will really take off in a few years, you mark my words. Every dog has its day as they say, but some old pros leave a lasting impression, if you'll pardon the pun."

"Ha ha, Robert—impression, I get it!" Kim laughed and noted with interest that Robert, himself was very knowledgeable about what was happening in the music world although the Premier Plus Agency dealt with all types of artistes, from opera singers and pop stars to illusionists and circus acts. "Are you telling me Oasis and Michael Jackson will disappear from the scene when the public stop buying their records?" she asked. "I love them and can't imagine the music industry being the same without them."

"Some artistes have been, and will be, at the top of the tree for a lifetime. Others will be one hit wonders. You only have to look at Cliff Richard. He and others like him still have what appeals to the young people of today, but those same young people are fickle and change their allegiance like they change their socks."

"Well, that makes them safe then. My brother doesn't change his socks very often," Kim quipped. "But I will find out as much as

I can. Cliff Richard has a big following of middle-aged women. My mum still loves him. How sad is that?" She grinned at Robert and thrilled at the thought of her new life. "I promise you, Rob, I'll make you proud of me. With you as my mentor, the world of entertainment will be my oyster. I'm really going to enjoy this job."

~ * ~.

The Royal Theatre in Bolton was eventually taken over by the local amateur operatic and dramatic groups as a permanent venue for their productions. The Manchester office closed and in 1993, surprising those around her, particularly her parents, Kim made the ambitious decision to invest in the Premier Plus Agency in London when Theo decided to retire. Robert went to be his live-in partner.

"I didn't see that coming," she told her boyfriend, Rick, when he met her at the office the day the company was officially handed over to her.

"What?" Rick asked.

"Robert and Theo. I knew they were gay, but they certainly didn't show any affection for each other in front of me. I don't think I ever saw them leave the office together. I just assumed they led separate lives."

"Whatever floats their little boat, Kim," he said dismissively. "How do you feel now you're the big boss? Will I have to make an appointment to see you?" Rick had met Kim at a George Michael gig two years before and he had been a regular visitor to her Chelsea flat ever since.

With a forced arrogant flick of her head, she replied cheekily, "Maybe."

~ * ~

All that had been five years ago and Kim's agency had flourished. She worked hard, travelled Europe extensively and had some of the best British artistes on her books that relied on her to find the best venues and the best deals. She established herself as an influential part of the entertainment industry. She had moved into Willow Bank just before the property market was set to boom. "Buy now, Kim," her friends in the property world advised her. "There are a lot of bargains to be had if you are prepared to renovate."

She found Willow Bank in a sorry state, but within three months and with the services of a good builder and interior designer, she had created the perfect home for herself by the time she was twenty-nine. She kept her Chelsea flat for when she needed to be in the City on late nights at work. She was part of the London scene and rarely went back to Bolton where she had lived for most of her life as she was growing up.

~ * ~

She stood on her deck and looked downstream from her Thames riverside home. She leaned on the wrought iron rail and sighed deeply, a long, need-to-relax sigh. Rick crept up behind her and wrapped his arms around her as he nuzzled her hair. "Marry me, Kim?" he asked quietly.

"Please, don't start that again, Rick. Not now," she said, her weary tone not hiding how she felt. "Don't spoil my daydream."

"I won't give up, you know, however much you try to delay the inevitable."

"There's nothing inevitable about it. I won't have you organising my life for me. Nobody will ever tell me what to do. I'll find my own way in life when I decide what it is I'm looking for. That missing *je ne sais quoi* is still proving to be very elusive."

Rick was irritated and he sighed audibly. "My, my, Miss Mason, that's a very bold statement and somewhat arrogant, if I might make so bold, but I've heard it all before, Kim, and your reasoning doesn't stack up. How can you hang on to the notion that something isn't quite right with your life on mere intuition?

It's illogical and totally out of character for you. You're a successful businesswoman, for goodness sake—organised beyond doubt, methodical to the point of fanatical, so strategic you could come a close second to Field Marshall Montgomery and on-the-dot punctual in everything you do." He smiled cynically. "That just about puts being the typical bride out of reach for you then. You would never allow yourself to be late!"

"Stop it, Rick. Change the subject, or you will find yourself going home without dinner," she said pointedly.

"That's another thing..."

"And don't bring up the moving in here issue again," Kim told him. "I'm not ready for the full twenty-four seven commitment yet. If you're not happy with the weekend arrangement we have, then you know what to do." She turned away from him and stared out at the beautiful view down the river again, the weeping willows swaying gently in the evening breeze and the water lapping at the sloping grassy banks. "Now you've ruined what promised to be a blissful evening. I hope that makes you happy," she said, not attempting to hide her feelings.

"Oh, that's so typical of you, Kim. Blame me for everything; blame me for being in love with you, for wanting to spend the rest of my life with you; blame me for still being here in your life in spite of continuous rejection and..." He paused. "... and blame me when you are a frustrated, lonely old maid still thinking that something isn't quite right with your life. I'm going to be thirty years old next month and forgive me, Miss Mason, if I've come to the point in *my* life when I want to settle down and have a family of my own. If you won't marry me, then there isn't anything left to discuss...and yes, I will go home without dinner." He stalked off upstairs to collect his belongings and left without saying goodbye. When the door slammed in his wake, Kim returned to the deck to mull over what had just happened.

Later, she lay on her bed staring up at the ceiling. *Why am I so calm?* she thought. *I'm usually angry with the whole world if Rick and I argue. But we didn't actually argue—I merely told him to stop interfering and trying to organise my life.* She took in a deep breath, her lips tightly shut as she assessed the stance she felt she had to make. *Mum always says I'm too independent for my own good, but then Dad usually comes out with some pearls of wisdom like: 'The greatest gifts you can give your children are the roots of responsibility and the wings of independence.'* She smiled in acceptance of her father's affection. *Dear Dad, I can't remember him ever raising his voice to me and I know I would never want to do anything that would damage our wonderful relationship. He is the best, the absolute best.* She breathed in deeply again and let out a long, meaningful sigh. *And now, as far as Rick is concerned...* She shrugged nonchalantly...*que sera, sera,* and yet her minor run-in with him had irritated her. *I like him,* she thought, *but I don't love him. I can't agree to marry him on those terms. It would be a disaster. One-sided love affairs never work. I just have to finish with him and I guess I'll have to risk his being devastated when I tell him. Even so, I'll have to tell him. I'm certainly not ready for the big, elaborate wedding...* Suddenly, a childhood memory filled her mind. She was dressed in pink and was walking along a red carpet towards a man and a lady who were getting married, people whose faces or names she couldn't recall. *I know I felt very important, but why the hell had we travelled all that way just for me to be a bridesmaid?*

~ * ~

December 1974

They arrived at the airport very early in the morning and met Auntie Penny and Uncle Gerry. Baby Robert was fast asleep in his buggy as was her little brother, Anthony. She clung tightly to her daddy's hand and wondered what it was going to be like to fly way up in the sky. "Will it be scary, Daddy?" she asked. "What if I need the toilet when we're up there in the sky? Are the toilets outside the aeroplane?"

Ben looked down at his beautiful, wide-eyed daughter and smiled. "You'll be fine, sweetheart. There are toilets inside the plane and you'll love looking through the clouds and seeing all the tiny houses below. Everything looks tiny from up in the air."

"Will we see our house?" Kim asked.

"No, but we might see Windsor Castle when we leave Heathrow," her mum chipped in. "That's where the Queen lives."

"Just think, everybody," Gerry rejoined cheerily, "Kevin Keegan might be on our flight to London. Liverpool play Arsenal this weekend."

"Don't be daft, Ger. They'll go down to London in the club coach," Penny told him as she nudged him in the ribs.

"Just imagine though," Gerry continued. "It'd make my day just to be breathing the same air as King Kev for an hour."

Kimberley looked up at the ardent Kevin Keegan fan and said, "You're just being silly, Uncle Gerry, and there's only you who supports Liverpool anyway. We support Bolton Wanderers, don't we, Daddy?"

"All right, little Miss Smarty Pants," Gerry said, winking at his close friends. "What would you say if Peter Reid was on the plane? He's a Scouser anyway. We've only lent him to Bolton till he realizes the best team is in his home town."

Belinda shook her head and smiled. "Ever the same Gerry," she said. "But we love you just the way you are."

During most of the long, tedious flight from London to Singapore, the three children slept. Belinda and Penny sat together, intermittently trying to nap, but generally awake and listening to the drone of the massive engines that were carrying them to a place none of them ever dreamed they would go. Penny looked Belinda squarely in the eye. "Tell me honestly, Bel, are you okay with this?"

"With what? The flight?" Belinda asked in reply.

"Stop evading the issue. I know you too well, Belinda Robinson." She used Belinda's maiden name to emphasise the point she was making. "You are travelling to Australia to attend the wedding of your ex-boyfriend…"

"He was never my boyfriend, Pen."

"Well," Penny continued quietly, yet pointedly, "I didn't want to be so brutally honest, but you give me no choice." She lowered her voice to a theatrical whisper. "We are going to see the father of your little girl get married. How do you feel?"

"Ben is Kimberley's father, Penny. That's all you need to remember." Belinda was deliberately forthright.

"All right, but don't be stoical just because you've built this invisible, protective wall around yourself. I'm here if you need me and we all love you, Ben especially."

"I know and I really do love him. I'm with the right man, Pen, and we haven't needed to discuss the present situation because we both know how we feel. We simply do not discuss anything to do with Joel Winston. When this trip is over, we'll never mention his name again."

Penny wasn't so sure the situation was so simple, but she had to accept that this was the way Ben and Belinda had dealt with it all along. "Okay, Bel, if that's how you want it, I won't mention it again and we do owe this trip to the kindness of Mrs. Winston. She really must have changed and I guess that's down to Joel taking her out to Australia."

"Yeah, I guess so," Belinda agreed. "I prefer to forget the one and only time I met her on the landing at Maggie's shop. Jeez! I bet she'd like to forget that little episode, too."

"But she knows about Kim, doesn't she?" Penny asked.

"Oh yes. She was very understanding when she phoned. She spoke to Ben first and apologised for how she treated him when he was growing up. He told her it wasn't necessary to apologise, but she said she needed to do it for herself. She had to try to clear her conscience before she started her new life with Doctor Flynn."

"We won't bear grudges then, Bel. Let's just wish her all the best," Penny said gently.

"When she spoke to me, she wanted to reassure me that she would always accept Ben as Kimberley's daddy. That's all that was necessary for me, especially knowing how she was with Joel," Belinda revealed. "I'm happy with that."

"That's it then," Penny concluded. "Life goes on! I still think it's outrageous that Joel is getting married and he doesn't know! The Joel we knew would never have allowed that to happen. The whole point of him being in Liverpool was because his mother kept interfering, wasn't it? Well, she's interfered big time now. It's taken Gerry all his time not to give any hints in his letters of what is happening. I have to say, though, Joel surprises me with the way he's kept in touch with Gerry."

"Ben reckons he's changed," Belinda pointed out. "He says, according to your Gerry's version, the girl Joel's marrying has sorted him out. Tall order, I'd say, but good luck to them."

Penny grinned at her best friend. "We're going to Australia!" she enthused. "Who would believe it?"

~ * ~

The eight-year-old Kimberley had slept intermittently on that long flight and wakened several times to hear her mummy and Auntie Penny talking about her daddy. The twenty-nine year-old Kimberley was strangely recalling something she hadn't thought about for well over twenty years. *Why am I suddenly remembering this? I don't remember anything at all about Australia and my parents have never mentioned it once in all the years since. That is very strange —very, very strange.*

~ * ~

January 1975

Leaving the idyllic Australian summer behind, Ben and Belinda Mason returned home to wintry Bolton with their children, Kimberley and Anthony, to frozen snow and icy winds. The contrast of the climates was not lost on them. They had just spent a relaxed holiday in the sun and as they landed in Manchester, they inwardly felt the chill. They shivered at the harsh decisions that had to be made. "Our lives will change forever," Belinda stated. "We have to be determined about this, Ben." Her tone was cold, almost bitter.

"I know that, Bel, but there are other people involved and how can we be sure they will be as determined as we are to block Joel Winston from our lives?" Ben said pointedly. "We really can't tell other people what to do."

"Penny and Gerry are our best friends…"

"But Gerry is Joel's close friend too and they have kept in touch regularly since Joel went to Australia. From what I can gather, they don't discuss us and that's fine. Kimberley is never mentioned either so we have to be happy with that. For what it's worth, I think we can trust Joel not to interfere in our lives. He always respected the demands I made of him when you fell pregnant." Ben was trying to encourage Belinda to place some trust in the boy she was determined to hate forever.

"Don't ask me to like him," she said bluntly, "because I'll never do that."

Ben took hold of her hand and looked directly into her eyes. "I'm not asking anything of the kind. I'm delighted you don't like him, if you want the truth. I need to know it's me you love and not him," Ben told her sincerely. "All that aside, I made my peace with him when we bought their house. I really feel no animosity towards him anymore."

"Well, I do and the sooner we adhere to our rules, the better I'll like it," Belinda said forcefully.

"Well, we'd better set the ground rules before we see Penny and Gerry," he told her. "I'm not sure how they'll respond, especially since we have all just spent three delightful weeks in Australia due to the kindness of Mrs. Winston…" He paused, realising his mistake. "Mrs. Flynn, now."

Belinda gave him a wry smile. "I know that and I appreciate what she did for us, but in all honesty, those three days in Perth were sheer agony for me." There was a lot of bitterness in her tone and Ben was surprised at the depth of her feelings.

"My goodness, Bel," he said, "Even I didn't know you felt so bad about it. You must have put on a brilliant show and how come you're only now telling me how you felt? I'm your husband and I would have thought I'd notice if you were uncomfortable in Joel's company."

"Ben!" she remonstrated. "You have to get used to not uttering that name to me, or to anybody else. The name must never be mentioned in this house and whenever we are with Penny and Gerry. That's the rule. And there is to be no mention ever again of Australia. Kim must not hear us talking about any of those things wherever we are. Promise me; you have to promise me, Ben," she pleaded with more than a hint of desperation in her voice.

"I promise, but we can't completely carry out our plans until we've spoken to the Connollys.

~ * ~

A couple of months passed before Belinda and Ben were ready to meet up with Penny and Gerry. Belinda telephoned. "We haven't spoken for ages, what with jobs and things. How are you fixed for going to Chester Zoo on Saturday?" Belinda asked. "The children will love it and we can catch up later at our place. Do you fancy staying over on Saturday night?"

"I'll have to check with Gerry. If Liverpool are at home, it will be a no-no. He won't go to the zoo instead of Anfield. It's more than my life's worth to even suggest it," Penny said amiably. "It sounds good to me though. We haven't seen you since we got back from Australia."

Belinda cringed, but let it go. "Well, let me know as soon as possible and then we can finalise our plans."

~ * ~

The visit to the zoo was a great success with the children and they all went back to Bolton as arranged. Once the children were in bed, Penny announced her news. "I'm pregnant again!"

"Congratulations!" Ben said enthusiastically. "We're delighted for you, aren't we, Bel? That calls for a toast."

"I wondered why you have been drinking soft drinks all day," Belinda told her friend.

"I've got this massive thirst. It happened when I was expecting Robbie too," Penny divulged. "I have a passion for Florida orange juice."

"At least it's not for pickled onions," Gerry quipped. "I hate to tell you what onions do to her…"

"But you're going to tell anyway, aren't you, dear?" Penny interrupted. "They make my breath smell…"

"And the rest, Pen!"

"Oh, shut up, Ger. Nobody wants to know that," she chastised him amicably.

Gerry had to have the last laugh. "If Penny suddenly decides she has a craving for onions, just make sure you have a few pegs available for your noses."

They all laughed as Penny cast a look of disapproval at her joker husband.

Ben brought the proceedings under control. "Here's to Gerry and Penny and the next little Connolly."

Suddenly there was an awkward silence. "Wow, Ben. That was a conversation killer," Gerry quipped again.

"Not as long as you're in the room, Gerry, but we do need to talk to you both about something serious," Ben told them. "Let's go in the lounge."

"Nothing wrong, I hope," Penny said looking closely at her best friend for any signs of distress.

Ben took in a long, deep breath. "Nothing wrong as such, but...sit down...please." He motioned to them to sit on the settee.

Belinda made herself comfortable at Ben's feet as he sat in his favourite chair and she spoke first. "Ben and I have been discussing this for weeks and before he starts, I would like you to know this is for me and for Kim. You are our best friends and I hope you'll understand." She smiled weakly and signalled to Ben to begin.

Penny took hold of Gerry's hand for reassurance. "You are making me nervous," she said to Ben.

"You've no need to be nervous, Pen. We just have a big favour to ask of you."

"Ask away," Gerry told them. "What are friends for?"

Ben took in another deep breath. "You know and we know you have always kept the secret about Kim's paternity since Bel found out she was expecting?"

The Connollys nodded cautiously.

Ben continued. "What we are going to ask you now is really just an extension of that secret." He paused as he detected curious expressions on his friends' faces. "Kim must never hear Joel's name—ever. Nor must she be reminded she was in Australia to be a bridesmaid."

Penny looked at him incredulously. "But she's an eight-year-old child. How can you stop her thinking about everything that happened in Australia?"

"We can't get into her mind, but we haven't mentioned anything about it since we arrived home. When she got over the jetlag and opened her Christmas presents which were waiting for her, she was too involved with her new pocket calculator..."

"You've bought her a calculator?" Gerry was aghast. "She'll never learn her times-tables now! We never had calculators. I think they're ridiculous!"

"Please, Gerry, let me finish," Ben urged. "We are astonished ourselves that she hasn't mentioned the trip once since we arrived home. For an eight year old, that's quite something, but she has had so many distractions. We also bought her a portable tape recorder with earphones and she listens to Stevie Wonder and Abba all the time. We've been to see *Herbie Rides Again* and she pestered us rotten to see *Babes In The Wood* at Manchester Palace because two of her friends from her dancing school are playing the babes."

"How can you be so sure she won't bring up the trip when she's over her presents and her outings?" Penny asked pointedly.

"We can't, but in addition to all that, she had school work to catch up and her piano lessons. Her little mind is so full of other things, we can only pray she forgets very quickly," Belinda added.

"To be frank," Penny continued, "I think you're asking a lot of a child, but what is it you want from us?"

Ben looked at them squarely. "We'd like you to promise never to speak of Joel and Australia ever again when you are in our company..."

"That's a hard ask, Ben. Joel is my mate and it took a long time to get our relationship back on track," Gerry told them. "I'm not stopping being his mate even for you and Kimberley. Sorry."

Belinda turned to look at her husband, to try to read his reaction. "Please, Gerry," she pleaded as her gaze returned to her friends. "Kimberley must never know who her father is. She must always think Ben is her daddy. The only way we can do that is by blocking all thoughts of Joel and Australia..." She paused because just saying the two words made her feel sick to the stomach. "...We must block all thoughts from our minds. Those words must never be uttered in our house, or in our presence."

Penny wiped away the tears that had involuntarily coursed down her cheeks. "Oh, Bel," she said with sincerity. "We'll never let you down, you know that, but it's going to be so difficult. There were *some* good times with him..." She deliberately didn't say his name. "...for Gerry in particular, but we've kept your secret for nine years so we're not going to broadcast it now."

Gerry was pensive. He sighed deeply. "For the sake of our friendship, I'll do as you ask. I'll not speak about you or Kimberley when I speak to our Aussie friend, but I can't stop being his mate."

"What if he asks about us?" Ben enquired.

"I don't think he will," Gerry explained. "In the past nine years, he hasn't asked about any of you. I think that's how he deals with the situation, so in that respect, I guess you both have the same thoughts."

"Thanks for that," Ben said. "We have to think what we're doing is right for us and for Kim."

"Okay, mate. Consider it done."

Three

Kim didn't hear from Rick for weeks. "I'm not going to call him," she told Melissa, her personal assistant. "He knows where I am if he feels inclined to get in touch, but I won't have him telling me what to do."

"Aren't you being a tiny bit harsh, Kim?" Melissa reproached her. "The guy asked you to marry him. That's hardly telling you what to do."

"I know," Kim retaliated, "but that's just it. A girl has the right to say no, hasn't she? He knows how I feel and he keeps on constantly pushing the marriage thing. Why can't we just carry on doing what we're doing?" She grinned at the bemused Melissa. "He got his leg over every weekend!"

The two young women laughed, but Melissa looked Kim in the eye and said sarcastically, "Well, what more could a guy want?"

"You're married, Mel. How did you feel about Paul when he proposed to you?"

Melissa placed the large ledger she was holding on the desk and sighed deeply. "I loved him with every fibre of my being," she said dreamily. "We had been going out for two years and we didn't have sex until our wedding night…"

"You didn't have sex?" Kim exclaimed. "Flippin' heck, Melissa, I thought everybody had sex these days as soon as it becomes legal. My mother would think you were perfect. For some unfathomable reason, she's got a massive hang-up as regards sex before marriage. She'd go spare if she knew my first time was in Magaluf when I was seventeen. It was a holiday romance with a Spanish waiter, a Julio Iglesias look-alike. I'm telling you, Mel, he was amazing…"

"That explains it then. You've nothing to look forward to. Do you think you are allowing that first sexual encounter to affect your judgment about marriage, Kim?" Melissa asked seriously.

"Lighten up, Mel. Of course I'm not allowing a teenage crush to affect my decisions now. Why would I need to do that?" Kim was feeling irritated with Mel and she inwardly chastised herself for feeling so strongly about a friendly enquiry. "Sorry," she said. "Let's just forget the whole damned business of Rick. There are more important things in my life. We have a meeting with the Albert Hall events manager tomorrow and I want to have all the information at my fingertips before then."

~ * ~

Back in Bolton, Belinda felt restless. "I need a project," she told Ben. "Something to keep me occupied on my days off."

"What sort of project? Community work? Altar flowers at church? The Women's Voluntary Service?" Ben asked, "And why now?"

Belinda thought for a moment. "I really don't know why now. I just need a distraction. I've been thinking about it for a couple of weeks, but nothing so impressive as community work and I don't want to do the altar flowers each week. There are regulars who do that and I don't think they'd take too kindly to my joining them out of the blue."

Ben nodded in appreciation of that. "I've attended that church since I was eleven years old, initially to get a place at St Luke's High School, but I hate to see the holier-than-thou attitude of some of the church stalwarts. Some people just diminish the whole meaning of Christianity. Why they have to be so judgmental, I don't know." He laughed at himself. "I sound like the pan calling the kettle black. I'm being a bit judgmental myself, aren't I?"

"Maybe you are, just a little bit, but I know what you mean. I don't think judgmental is a word I'd associate with you anyway, Ben," Belinda told him. "Nobody could ever call you that and I should know."

"What about the Women's Voluntary then?" He grinned mischievously at his wife.

"Excuse me, Ben Mason, but I don't regard myself as being old enough to be in the WVS, not yet anyway. I'm only forty-seven and being a little old lady seems to be the number one criterion to serve tea to hospital patients."

"A bit disparaging, Mrs. Mason, when those little old ladies as you call them, kept the servicemen and the country on their feet during and after the war," Ben told her, "but I do know what you mean."

Belinda suddenly came up with an idea. "I think I'll tidy the loft. We have a lifetime of belongings up there. We could give a lot of them to Oxfam. Not quite a community project, but we'll be helping a charity as well as clearing the house of unwanted things. I wouldn't exactly say it's junk, so somebody might have a use for it."

The telephone rang, interrupting their conversation. "I'll get it," Ben called as he left Belinda to contemplate her big clean-up.

He returned with a smile on his face. "It was Kim. She's coming home for the weekend."

"Is Rick coming with her?" Belinda asked, a look of uncertainty on her face. "I'm still not comfortable with them sharing a bed in our house..."

"Oh, come on, Bel. This is nineteen ninety-six and it's a fact of life these days that couples sleep together, married or not," he told her light-heartedly. "It was different in our day."

Belinda went quiet and stared down at her feet to hide her embarrassment.

"Sorry, sweetheart. I wasn't casting aspersions at you. It just happens these days and people don't worry about it. Please try to understand that every time Kim's sleeping arrangements are talked about, it doesn't highlight your past. I wish I knew how to reassure you that I love you and what happened with Joel..."

"Stop, Ben. I don't need you to explain that to me. I'm the one who has had to live with it for almost thirty years. Suddenly, it seems to be rearing its ugly head again and the more you go on about it, the more vivid those memories are. Just forget it, please."

"Okay, but you worry me sometimes. *You* obviously can't forget it and that's very sad. The modern concept of relationships should make you more at ease with your situation," Ben told her deliberately. "You can't hang on to the anger and guilt forever. I have never stopped loving you since that first night we met at the Connollys' place and later at the Cabin Club. Cilla Black was on, do you remember that? I thought you were with Joel, but he assured me you weren't. I knew you liked him, but I hoped you would learn to love me eventually. You're hanging on to all this bitterness because of that one afternoon and I have to say, it makes me wonder if it's Joel you still love and not me."

"I do love you, Ben. Why do I have to keep reminding you of that?" She was unreasonably irritated. "But I still have massive hang-ups about Kim; I always have. I love her for being *my* child, not Joel's. I have to admit it's very difficult not to see Joel every time I look at her. I want to see you in her, but I can't. She has his hair, his eyes and yes, his stubbornness and arrogance at times. I'm amazed she doesn't look in the mirror every morning and wonder where she came from. She isn't like me and she sure as hell will never be like you."

"I'm sure some of our characteristics have rubbed off on her," Ben said confidently. "Contrary to her super efficiency, she is certainly untidy like me and I know for a fact that Joel wasn't untidy...his mother would never have allowed it...and she has your endearing habit of sticking out her tongue when she's concentrating." He smiled affectionately at his wife. "Please don't stress, darling. Nothing has surfaced in twenty-odd years, so what on earth is going to cause it to surface now? And in answer to your question, no, Rick is not coming with her. I don't know what's going on there at all. She seemed almost dismissive when I asked about him."

Belinda moved nearer to her husband and held him close. "Hopefully she won't hop into bed with the next boy she meets, but thanks, Ben," she said.

"For what?"

"For being you; just for being you."

~ * ~

Belinda threw herself with gusto into the loft clean-up. She found boxes of birthday cards, Christmas cards, wedding cards, anniversary cards, new baby cards for both Kimberley and Anthony, all lovingly tied with pretty silk ribbon, "I'll throw out the Christmas cards," she said to her reflection in a dusty old dressing table mirror. "The others are our history so I can't throw those out. Kim and Tony will enjoy reading the loving messages one day." She placed the boxes on a shelf, mentally acknowledging things on the shelf were the 'to keep' collection. There were plastic bags full of baby clothes wrapped in tissue paper. She held each tiny dress and romper suit to her, savouring the fond memories of motherhood. "I really shouldn't hang on to these. They're old fashioned now." On her lap, she spread out a tiny cardigan and sweater she had spent hours knitting. "And young mothers don't want home-knits these days." She sighed. "Times do change. In my day, I spent nine months knitting and sewing and saving up to buy a pram. These days, they buy baby clothes from the high street stores, have top of the range prams on credit cards and have Cæsarean sections by choice. Are we breeding mothers who can't cope with natural childbirth?" She sighed again, more out of resignation than acceptance of the New Age mothers and reluctantly placed the bag to one side to be discarded.

By Saturday afternoon, she had sorted what she considered to be the wheat from the chaff. She piled up all the stuff that was to go to the charity shop and left it in the vestibule to be collected on Monday morning. Still in the loft, leaning against the old mirror was her guitar. She strummed a few chords in private and hummed a couple of songs from her repertoire until tears of sadness prevented her from continuing. Initially, it felt good to remember the familiarity of the instrument in her hands, but as she sang her favourite Elvis Presley song, *Can't Help Falling in Love,* albeit in whispered tones, she stopped abruptly. "Damn you, Joel Winston!" she cried and quickly returned the guitar to its case, ready to place it with the other rubbish in the charity shop pile.

Ben stood at the bottom of the stairs and listened. He sighed deeply, pushed his hands deep into his pockets and went quietly out of the door.

Four

In 1996, as Kimberley Mason was contemplating the possibilities of a future with Rick Kingsford in London, Doctor Sean Flynn and his wife, Nell, were happily relaxing in their Queensland home. When Sean retired, he and Nell sold their Sydney apartment and bought a house on the Coomera River, invested in a boat, *Lady Luck*, and spent many hours cruising the waterways of the Gold Coast. Nell had never returned to England, the land of her birth. Over breakfast on the terrace one morning, they talked of a visit to Sean's native Ireland, a trip that would take in England too and it caused Nell to feel anxious for the first time in over twenty years.

"I really have no desire to return to the UK," she told her husband. "That place holds so many bad memories for me. I feel nervous just thinking about it."

"Darling Nell," Sean said. "Why would you feel like that after such a long time? I thought we had exorcised the ghosts of the past."

"We have...*I* have," she corrected, "but I don't want to return to a place where I succumbed to a life of...well, to put it bluntly, a life of booze and debauchery that disgusts me even to think about it."

Sean regarded her with confused feelings. "Sweetheart, those are such horrible words and words I will never associate with you. We have been married for almost twenty-one years, all very happy years, where we have never harked back to the past. It hasn't been necessary, because we both wanted—correction, *needed* —our life together to be a brand new start for us both. Why on earth would you want to bring all this to light again now?"

Nell looked at the man who was her husband, her lover, her friend, the man who had rescued her from the brink of despair, not once, but twice. "I don't know why, darl. Just recently in quiet moments, I have been reminiscing a bit. Maybe it comes with growing older. Unfortunately, thinking back has allowed unpleasant memories to surface. Even my dreams are full of the things I would prefer to forget. I wake up with my heart pounding in my chest and there is always something looming at the end, something intangible, something I can't reach, something that seems to be cut off from me."

"Like what?" Sean asked.

"That's just it, I don't know. I always wake up frustrated that I don't know what it is that's hiding from me. You know what dreams are like. They can be so infuriating."

Sean smiled affectionately. "Just forget them, Nell," he advised. "That's all they are, dreams, not reality."

Nell listened, but she wasn't so sure and her dreams had indeed reluctantly transported her back to Bolton...

~ * ~

"Wake up, you great oaf. I don't want you here in my bed. I don't want you in my house. Get up and get out!" she screamed, her head pounding with every word she uttered. She hastily picked up his grubby clothes, and throwing them at him, she

shouted again, "Come on, Mr whoever you are. Get out of my house —NOW!"

Stan was slowly coming round. "You weren't saying that last night, you little tart. You couldn't wait to let me into your posh knickers."

"Don't be so obnoxious! I don't know how you got here, but you'd better leave before I call the police." Nell was beside herself.

"All right, all right, I'm going, lady. Don't get yer knickers in a knot," and he rumbled around the bedroom repulsively breaking wind as he bent to pick up his clothes. "Can I have a cup o' tea before I leave?" he asked the distraught Nell.

"OUT!" she yelled and hung on to her head in order to stop the incessant throbbing in her temples as she followed him down the stairs.

Stan glared at her and wobbled to the foot of the stairs, puffing and panting as though he'd just run a marathon. As he opened the door, he turned and said, "A word of advice, lady. Don't offer yourself on a plate if you don't want a man to have his fill. You were gagging for it last night. But thanks, missus. You were a good lay!" He grinned sickeningly and closed the door behind him with a flourish...

~ * ~

"Nell?" Sean took hold of her hand across the table. "You were miles away."

She shuddered. "Yes, I was. Can we go out on *Lady Luck*? I need to feel the wind on my face, to blow away the cobwebs. Maybe we can stop at Sanctuary Cove for lunch. I'd like that."

Sean was never happier than when he was in charge of *Lady Luck*. Nell often stood by his side as they glided through the clear, blue waters when the sun shone bright in a cloudless sky. Today she sat astern, her sun-lounger facing where she could watch the frothy waters part in their wake. *This is bliss,* she thought dreamily. *What more could I wish for at my time of life?* She closed her eyes and felt the gentle rock of *Lady Luck* as they cruised along the Broadwater towards Sanctuary Cove.

~ * ~

"I'm surprised to see you in here," the woman said. "I'd heard you were too posh and stuck up to be seen in a pub, especially in the town centre."

"Look, lady, I don't know who you are, but sit down and have a drink. I feel like a bit of woman talk. Makes a change from the sleazebag men who usually talk to me. Pull up a chair," Nell invited her would-be companion.

"Don't mind if I do, seeing as you're paying," the woman said. "I'm Connie, Connie Mason."

Nell looked at Connie through squinting eyes. The wine was taking effect and she found it difficult to focus. "Hello then, Connie. I know somebody called Mason, but I can't think of his first name."

"Ben?" Connie asked her.

"That's it! How did you know that?" Nell nudged her new friend and laughed. "You must be psychic. Clever thing, aren't you?"

"Not clever, dear. He's my son, not that he has anything to do with me these days. He moved out as soon as he left school. I never got so much as a penny from his wages, the little toe-rag. And now he's leading our Michael away too."

"Don't tell me about wayward sons. I've got one who can't bear even to talk to me," Nell divulged between drinking down the remains of the bottle and ordering another.

"Looks like we understand each other," she told Connie. By the time they had had several glasses of wine each, the two women were ready to survey the landscape.

"Look to your right," Connie instructed. "I don't fancy yours!" and she laughed raucously.

The two men were smiling at them and beginning to move in their direction.

"I'll have the one in the white shirt. Ooh, look at his rippling muscles." Nell smiled at him invitingly.

Waking up the next morning with the rippling muscles next to her turned out to be more like lying next to rolls of blubber. Nell felt violently sick and grabbed the waste bin so as not to throw up on her bedroom carpet. As she staggered to the bathroom, she heard voices coming from her guest room.

"Well, I didn't have to ask you twice if you fancied a bit of slap and tickle," the woman said.

"I must have had a few," the man replied. "God knows what the wife will say when I arrive home."

"Oh, just tell her you stayed at Jimmy's...that's your mate's name, isn't it?" the woman's voice continued. "I won't tell. Your secret's safe with me so long as you pay up."

"What? I'm not paying for what you offered me without having to ask, you cheeky mare." The man was outraged.

"Well, cough up, or I'll follow you home and tell yer wife myself." The woman's voice was raised now, almost at screaming pitch.

Nell stood motionless on her landing with her waste bin still in her hand. Her head was banging and she could not believe what she had just heard. "Who are these people?" she silently asked herself.

Creeping down the stairs and into the kitchen, she put on the kettle and waited for her uninvited guests to appear. When they did make an appearance, she eyed them incredulously. She vaguely recognised the woman. Struggling to remember the night before, she managed a smile and said, "Good morning," and as the three people entered, she recalled the woman's name. "Oh, Connie, isn't it?"

"Sure is, dear. Thanks for the bed. Lovely room too," Connie offered.

The two men looked uncomfortable. "I don't know you, I've never seen you, I will deny all of this if I ever see you again," the man who had been arguing with Connie said defiantly. "I'm off. Come on, Jimmy. We'll have a lot of explaining to do when we get home."

As the door banged shut, Connie grinned at Nell and waved two five pound notes in the air. "Good night," she said. "Bloody good night. Thanks, dear. We'll have to do it again sometime." She left without another word.

Nell's head hurt, but somehow she was unravelling the snippets of information that intermittently filtered into her confused mind. "Connie Mason," she remembered. "Oh my... Ben's mother, the reason I wouldn't allow Joel to bring Ben into this house." She shuddered at the thought that a woman like that had spent the night with a strange man in her guest room. "Oh my..." she said again, "and she took money from him. Oh my God, I need a drink."

~ * ~

Lady Luck's engines shuddered to a halt and Nell woke with a start.

Sean tied up the boat and helped Nell ashore. "Do you remember Ben who came to our wedding?" she asked.

"Vaguely. Why?"

"I was just thinking about him...well, truthfully, his mother really." She needed to talk about her recent anxieties, to give them air, to get them out into the open.

Sean sighed. "For goodness sake, Nell, you're like a dog with a bone," he told her, frustration evident in his tone. "Let it go, please," he pleaded. "All that's in the past and should be left there. Please don't bring up memories that obviously distress you. I really don't understand why you have suddenly started talking about it again. It's all so pointless."

"I don't understand it either, but I'm not sleeping well and all the restlessness seems to make me have weird dreams when I do fall asleep. Does that seem odd to you?" she asked and she shrugged as she deliberately forced a confused smile towards Sean who was looking totally bemused.

"Well, at least you can smile about it," he commented. "Come on, let's go to the yacht club for lunch. We'll have the seafood buffet and then relax with *Lady Luck* afterwards before we set off back."

"Sounds good to me," Nell replied and she made a bold effort to totally clear her mind of her embarrassing past. "Laughing at myself might just be the answer," she told him. *If only my past was funny.* "And don't forget, we must keep the next few days free to get ready for Joel and Sheralyn's visit."

Sean grinned. "You'll never change, Nell. Everything stops for Joel, but I love you for it. Leaving Joel to his own devices just wouldn't be on your agenda."

"I know," she admitted resignedly, "but I stopped interfering a long time ago. I promised Joel I would never again tell him what he should, or shouldn't, do and by the same token, he told me he'd never forgive me if I tried to organise his life for him again."

Sean nodded his head knowingly. "You handed that role over to Sheralyn twenty years ago. I reckon she has tamed Joel, and their kids are a credit to them."

Nell agreed. "That girl is perfect for him...*and,*" she paused for effect, "he chose her for himself."

~ * ~

"All you think about is yourself ..." She hesitated. "...after all I've done for you."

"You mean like choosing my A level subjects for me and going to beg for a job at the solicitor's office?" Joel spat the words in her direction. "Like making me have childish birthday parties and insulting my friends..." It sounded very futile, but how could he

relate all that had happened during the years of being dominated by a possessive, interfering mother who really didn't know her son at all?

"I never insulted your friends, Joel. How can you say that?"

"I can say it because it's true. You told me Ben couldn't come into our home, because you'd heard his mother had several boyfriends who stayed in her house at night, and you never welcomed Angela, or Amy, or Kate when they came to tea except to tell them I wasn't old enough to have a serious girlfriend. You made it pretty clear you disapproved of them. No wonder they dumped me soon afterwards," Joel told her.

"Well, they weren't good enough for you," Nell insisted.

"Who says?" Joel asked, *"And anyway, this is not about my friends, or whether you accepted them, it's about me doing what I want to do and in my own way. I'm not coming home.*

~ * ~

They strolled along the jetty, each with their own thoughts. "Where shall we sit?" Sean asked, interrupting Nell's reverie. "Inside or out?"

"Over there in the corner by the window. I can people-watch while I eat."

"You women!" her husband scoffed light-heartedly. "You are never satisfied until you are sitting in judgment of other people's idea of fashion."

"Whatever do you mean?" Nell asked coyly.

"You know very well what I mean and look who's here. Your partner in crime..."

"Hello, Gina. And Brian. How are you? Come and join us for lunch," Nell invited. *I need a distraction from the thoughts of my lurid past coming back to haunt me,* she thought. *Gina and Brian are just what I need right now.* They made room around the table for their friends, Nell's genial smile belying what was going on inside her head.

Five

The weekend with her parents in Bolton didn't happen for Kimberley. "Sorry, Mum, but something came up and I need to be in London."

"I understand," Belinda told her. "Theatrical agents lead busy demanding lives..."

"And you would know all about that, wouldn't you?" Kim said without thinking. Her tone was abrupt, even sarcastic.

Belinda was shocked. "What do you mean by that?" she retorted. "I was trying to be understanding, Kim, and may I remind you that sarcasm is the lowest form of wit..."

"But the highest form of intellect," Kim quipped, more light-hearted. "Sorry, Mum. I have a lot on my mind just at the moment."

"Anything your dad or I can help with?" she asked curiously, thinking, *She never did ask me about my flirtation with the entertainment industry in all the years she's been at Premier Plus.*

That's very odd, knowing what Kim's like, but I have to admit, I'm grateful she didn't.

"No," Kim replied. "I've been contacted by theatrical agents in Sydney. Apparently there's an Australian talent show that has uncovered the best things since sliced bread. The agent wants me to go over and have a look at a couple of groups with a view to bringing them over to the UK for exposure."

"Can't they send you demo discs? It's a long way to go just to have a look," Belinda said, desperately trying to keep anxiety out of her voice.

"No, I don't want demos; I want to see the real thing. That's how I've carried out my business from the start. I do listen to demo discs, but I like the live sound. I can't always make such massive decisions from recorded sound. If they can't sing live, then I'm usually not interested. Apart from that, there's one duo that does this amazing illusion act. They change costumes in seconds, literally seconds, so I have to see that live and in the flesh so to speak. I leave on Monday, eleven-thirty from Heathrow. I'll give you a call when I get back."

"When will that be?" Belinda asked, secretly thinking... *Hopefully you won't be there long enough to bump into people who know you.* "And what does Rick think about you jetting to the other side of the world at a moment's notice?"

"Rick isn't in the picture anymore," she said pointedly. "And I have no idea how long I'll stay. My ticket is open-ended. My visa lasts for three months so I might just have a look round, maybe go to Melbourne and Perth while I'm over there." She paused before she continued. "I hardly remember a thing about going to Australia before. How come we've never talked about it?"

Belinda was stunned and her heart was suddenly thumping in her chest. *Not now, Kimberley. Please not now.*

Fortunately for Belinda, Kim's train of thought moved on swiftly. "Melissa is running Premier Plus for me while I'm away. I know I can trust her to do everything my way." With that, she said a quick goodbye. "Gotta go, Mum. Love to Dad and love you."

"Love you too, sweetheart." *Please God keep her safe on the journey and...the rest doesn't bear thinking about.*

~ * ~

"But she's going to Perth," she cried. "How can you be so calm, Ben?"

Ben didn't know what to say. He thought carefully before he spoke. "We'll just have to hope she doesn't uncover any revelations while she's there, other than the ones she's gone to see. Think positive, Bel. Australia's a big place. What are the odds of her bumping into Joel?"

Belinda sighed deeply. "I hope you're right,' she said resignedly. "I sincerely hope you are right."

~ * ~

It was Friday afternoon when it happened. Excitement about their success and the pure emotion of the situation overwhelmed their sensibilities. They kissed passionately for the first time and as their kisses became more urgent, more forceful, events took their natural course.

"That wasn't supposed to happen," Joel said as they scrambled to find their clothes to hide their nakedness.

Belinda looked stunned. "You didn't enjoy it?" she asked, confused at Joel's reaction.

"I didn't say that," Joel snapped, "but we're not an item."

"We could be," Belinda told him wistfully. "It's not as though we're complete strangers."

Joel looked at his musical partner. She was nice, kind, attractive and endearingly honest to the point of being forthright on occasions, but that was it. He felt no hint of sexual chemistry really. What had just happened was a heat-of-the-moment thing. "No, we're not strangers, certainly not now..." He paused in order to make sure the words came out right. "I like you Bel..."

"What makes me think there's a 'but' coming?" she said.

Joel looked at the girl whose attractive blue eyes showed a hint of desperation. "I don't want to get involved, Bel. I don't want to say that the last half hour was a mistake either, but it was a one off."

Belinda snatched up her bag and headed for the door. "You posh boys are all the same. Think you are God's gift and every girl is yours for the taking. Well, stuff you, posh Joel." She opened the door and ran down the stairs, hot tears misting her view.

~ * ~

She woke with a start, breathing heavily. She stretched out her right arm to feel her husband sleeping quietly by her side. She turned over and snuggled close to him.

"What's this?" Ben asked sleepily.

"I just need to feel close to you. Go back to sleep." Belinda felt the warmth of his body and the comfort of his love, but try as she might, she herself, could not get back to sleep.

Six

Joel Winston and his family were planning to visit his mother in Queensland. After his marriage to Sheralyn in 1974, he had settled happily in their South Perth riverside home where they had three children, Glenn, Helena and Jasmine. Glenn at nineteen was very much the big brother to Helena, sixteen, and little Jasmine who was eleven. Joel had just celebrated his forty-eighth birthday and was contemplating his future.

"What shall I do about this job offer?" he asked his wife when she arrived home from the hospital where, after years of working on the wards, she had become chief administrator. This allowed her a nine to five day and every weekend off.

"I think you should take it, darl. You really don't want to be an ageing entertainer who looks as though he's past his use-by date!" She grinned at the man who had, eventually, turned out to be the best husband she could have wished for.

"Watch it, Mrs Winston!" he said to his wife and he laughed with her at the thought of his becoming a grey-haired pop idol. "DP once joked that I might be the next Cliff Richard, but I don't think I could ever walk in his shoes. You remember my tutor, Dafydd Powell, don't you?" His eyes misted over at the thought that his beloved DP was no longer alive. "I loved that guy." He sighed deeply. "Australian TV has been good to me, but I know when it's time to move on."

"I don't know why you're asking me what you should do, because you always do your own thing anyway. If it's one thing I have learned about you in the past twenty-two years, it's never to interfere with what you are doing. Your mum did warn me well in advance of our wedding!"

Joel smiled and went to sit on the deck overlooking the river. This had become a place of quiet contemplation and whenever Sheralyn saw him sitting alone, she knew to leave him for a while.

~ * ~

Joel had been into college to tie up the loose ends and he had a cup of tea ready for her as soon as she walked in.

"I'm sorry if I upset you, Mum, but I really did hate the course." He was trying to make his mother understand how he felt and his basic upbringing in being mannerly had not completely deserted him. "My heart wasn't in it and I couldn't see where it was leading. I want more out of life than going along with the flow just because the current is forcing me in that direction."

Nell smiled. "Very eloquently put, Joel," but she stopped him before they got into a heavy discussion about the rights and wrongs of his actions. She needed to choose her words carefully so Joel wouldn't accuse her of interfering again. She needed to be the very epitome of diplomacy. "The problem has been solved, Joel. You won't be swimming against the tide any longer," she told him. Joel listened as she explained the situation. She looked directly at him, trying to read the changing expressions on his face as she related her morning's exploits. At one point, she almost gave up, seeing what she thought was a look of extreme bitterness in his eyes.

She still continued to try to justify her actions until Joel suddenly stood up in disbelief, his arms flapping up and down as if he were about to take flight.

"Why have you done all that? You've made it look as though I'm a cretin who can't speak up for himself. That's twice now and for all I know, it may be more! For crying out loud, stop interfering in my life, Mother," and with that he stormed out and up to his bedroom.

She heard his heavy footsteps on the stairs and felt the whole house was coming down upon her. He grabbed a rucksack from the back of his wardrobe and put in as many of his clothes as he could manage. He had to get away. If he were to prove his worth in this world, he would do it on his own without his mother looking over his shoulder. He would stay at Ben's tonight and start his quest tomorrow. Then he smiled to himself ironically. He recalled what his mother had said about tomorrows, but told himself, "My tomorrow will come. Just you wait and see."

Nell was beside herself. When Joel came downstairs with his rucksack and his guitar strung over his shoulder, a look of complete defiance in his eyes, she pleaded with him to reconsider. She grabbed hold of her little boy and begged him not to go.

"Where will you go? What will you do?" she implored until the tears prevented her from presenting a logical argument for him to stay.

"I'll go to Ben's tonight," he told her. He owed her that at least. "And then I'll decide what I am going to do in my own time."

"But...."

"No buts, Mother." He knew she hated that formal title, but he felt so estranged from her at that moment that any words of endearment would diminish the depth of his true feelings. She had to know he was determined to stand alone on this and if it meant hurting her feelings in the process, then so be it. He was not falling for the guilt trip thing again. "You have to accept that I am no longer a child," he told her. "I have to demand that you respect my decision this time. I can't stand all this interference and the sooner you realise that, the better." They were strong words aimed at having an impact that should not be taken lightly and Nell felt the full force of his onslaught.

"You're being too sensitive, Joel. You are just like your father."

"Don't you dare use my dad to make me feel guilty! That's typical of you, Mother. Never your fault. You're always right and woe betide anybody who disagrees with your decision."

~ * ~

After a while, Sheralyn quietly approached him on the deck. She stood behind him, gently put her arms around him and nuzzled his hair. "Can I do anything to help, darl?" she asked.

"I was just thinking about what you said," he told her. "You know, I have never liked anybody telling me what to do. It almost destroyed Mum and me when I was growing up. She and I are too much alike and the friction between us was inevitable. I don't want our kids to be like that."

"But you're not so obsessed like your mum was," Sheralyn reassured him, "and we work together on our parenting. Unfortunately, when your dad passed away, he couldn't be there for you, otherwise your life would perhaps have been a whole lot different."

"I guess you're right, but forget all that stuff. I've made a decision."

"Alleluia!"

"Don't be facetious, Sher. I'm going to take the job offer. Working as an agent for up and coming artists will be a welcome change. I've done the hard yards in the spotlight and I have lots of experience with which to guide others along the rocky road to success. The Perth branch of the Obertelli Theatrical Agency has materialized just at the right time for me. I haven't been in contact with Shane Obertelli for years."

Sheralyn gave him a hug. "And you made that decision *all* on your own," she teased.

"Ah yes, but I knew you'd approve and that's the difference."

"Well, Mr. Winston, sir, might I use my wifely influence and ask you to sort out the clothes you want to take to Queensland? I'll sort out the kids' clothes, although the girls will want to choose their own, I'm sure. Glenn just needs boardies and thongs and he'll be happy, but I'll have to *interfere...*" She emphasized the word to make a flippant point. "...and make sure he has smart trousers and a clean shirt in case the Flynns take us to Palazzo Versace or The Sheraton Mirage for dinner."

Joel grabbed her hand and pulled her onto his lap. "Remember the first time I did this?" he asked with a glint in his eye.

"I sure do, baby," Sheralyn replied. "That was the day we fell in love and you sang your song *I'm Looking for Love* to me. How appropriate it was."

"Yes, it was, darl," and he broke into song again, quietly, but very meaningfully.

'I'm looking for love,
For the love of my life,
I need to feel loved and adored.
I'm looking for love,
For the romance of dreams,
Just being with you, I want more

Than a fleeting hello.
Please say those three words
'I love you' to me
And then I'll be perfectly sure...'

"Love conquers all, darling," she said tenderly.

Joel took her in his arms and kissed her; a long, loving kiss that showed her exactly how he still felt.

Seven

After the long flight from Heathrow to Sydney, Kim Mason gave herself a couple of days to recover before she sought out Simon Obertelli at the Head Office of the Obertelli Theatrical Agency, OTA. He had been given the task of introducing her to his colleagues. His father and owner of OTA was Shane Obertelli, previously based in Melbourne. The ageing show-biz impresario who now lived in Sydney was gradually handing over the business to his younger son. "This young girl has made quite a reputation for herself in London. She comes highly recommended by Theo Pendennis. I never met the guy, but we exchanged a few artists over the years. You look after her, son, and then we'll sort out the new office in Perth."

Kim found the office just off George Street. The receptionist, a very attractive young lady, Kim noticed, looked over her glasses at the woman who walked through the door.

"Hi, I'm Kimberley Mason. I have an appointment with Simon Obertelli." She found herself raising the inflection at the end of her sentences. *What are you doing, Kim?* She silently rebuked herself. *You've only been in the country five minutes and you're imitating the locals!*

"Take a seat, Miss Mason…"

"Kim, please…"

"Okay, Kim. Simon will be out in a minute," the receptionist said. She appeared to be closely scrutinizing Kim. "You know, you remind me of somebody and I can't think who. It'll come to me eventually."

"I hope it's somebody you liked, otherwise you might think I've come back to haunt you!" Kim grinned at the young woman and felt a kind of affiliation to her.

"A Pom with a sense of humour! Well, there's a first!"

"There are a few of us," Kim quipped and sat down. *Quit while you're ahead,* she thought.

After five minutes had passed, Simon Obertelli came out of his office. He moved forward almost as if it were urgent, offering his hand. "Hello, Kim. Good trip?"

His firm handshake made Kim feel at ease. "Good, but tiring. I took a couple of days off to recover." As she smiled, she caught sight of the receptionist in the corner of her eye. Her happy expression had been replaced by a scowl that Kim didn't understand. As Simon led her into his office, she looked directly at the receptionist and said, "Thank you."

The receptionist nodded, but her friendly smile had disappeared.

Simon Obertelli was very welcoming. "How are you finding Sydney?"

"Busy," Kim replied. "No, change that to manic. I thought London was very busy, but…well, it's nothing compared with this."

"That's just because you're not used to it. I guess I'd find London manic if I were ever to go there."

"Have you never been to the UK? You do surprise me. How come OTA knew about me then?"

"I have never been to the UK, but my dad has links with Theo Pendennis…"

"You're joking!" Kim exclaimed. "Theo never told me and when you called to invite me over, Theo's name wasn't mentioned. I just assumed it was a case of internet links. The wily old devil…"

"Who? My dad?" Simon asked smiling.

Kim smiled back and found her cheeks burning. "No, not at all. If you knew Theo, you would realise he would never want anybody to know he was interfering, even when he is actually being helpful. He's a firm believer in people finding their own way and he's also a very knowledgeable man who spots talent a mile away. It was his partner, Robert, who actually showed me the ropes."

"He obviously taught you well then," Simon said. "I like to think my dad has passed on his theatrical experience to me, too. He gained most of his expertise in television in Melbourne, but has a vast knowledge of the entertainment industry generally."

"Are you an only child?" Kim dared to ask.

"Why do you ask?"

"I just thought if it's a family concern, there would be other Obertellis involved and the staff list only has the two names," she explained.

"I'm not an only child. I have an older brother and a younger sister. My brother, Luigi —Lui for short, is an architect and has no interest in the entertainment industry other than being part of the audience at orchestral concerts. He's married with three children, twin boys and a girl. My mother spoils them rotten. They're her little *bambinos* and she's the typical Italian *nonna*. My sister, Bianca, lives in Italy with her Italian boyfriend. She's in real estate and sells million dollar mansions to rich foreigners." Simon was happy to share his family background with her. "What about you?"

Kim smiled. "Mine is the archetypal British family. Mother, father and two kids," she offered. "My dad is a bank manager, my mum is a beautician..." She paused. "I call her a hairdresser, but Dad always corrects me. My brother, Tony —Anthony really —is a maths teacher in a private school. He's saving up to get married and still lives at home with Mum and Dad—unheard of these days, but for some reason, my mum thinks the sun shines out of him because of it. That's just about it as regards my family."

"How about we go out to lunch before we start business?" Simon suggested as he got up from behind his desk and opened the office door. He called out to the receptionist. "I'm taking an early lunch, Janine. I'll be back by two o'clock. Tell any callers I'll contact them later. I'm going to show Kim a few of the sights of Sydney." He smiled amicably at his employee. "See you later."

"Yes, Mr. Obertelli," she replied and thought, *Hands off, lady. He's mine and don't get in my way.*

~ * ~

In Queensland, the Flynns and the Winstons were relaxing by the pool as the younger members of the family splashed around happily.

"Can you believe we'll be celebrating our twenty-first wedding anniversary this year?" Joel said. "Who'd have thought we'd be sitting by your pool in Queensland twenty-one years on?"

"To be sure, *I* can believe it," Sean told him. "I can believe anything after what's happened in my life. When I migrated to Sydney, I could never have envisioned all this. I'll never ever forget that phone call from Doctor Bertram..."

When the phone rang, he sighed. "I'm on holiday, for goodness sake," he said out loud. He snatched up the receiver. "Yes?" he snapped.

"Doctor Flynn?" When the answer was positive, the caller continued. "This is Doctor John Bertram from the Royal Perth Hospital. We have a serious leg injury from a road traffic accident and the son of the victim has requested that we call you to ask for your help. We don't have the expertise here and we told him so."

"Are you aware I'm on holiday, Doctor Bertram?" Sean informed him tersely.

"I'm so sorry, sir, but no, I wasn't aware of that. The hospital passed on your number and just said you weren't there today." John Bertram was embarrassed. "But the victim's son seems to know you."

"Oh I see, so who might he be?" Sean asked, suddenly made interested by this surprising piece of information. "I hadn't realised I knew anybody in WA."

"His name is Joel Winston, the TV star of the moment in these parts," Doctor Bertram informed him. "His mother, Nell, has been involved in a horrendous accident. Her right leg is shattered and we fear she may lose it without the necessary corrective surgery."

Sean was dumbfounded. Confused thoughts invaded his brain. Nell? In Perth? How come? It doesn't make sense.

"Doctor Flynn? Are you still there?" John Bertram asked.

Sean pulled himself together immediately. "I'll get the next flight out and come straight to the hospital. I'll phone when I know what time I land. Please have a car waiting for me," and he slammed down the receiver, not in temper, but in the unimaginable intensity of the moment.

~ * ~

"Are you still with us, Sean?" Nell asked. "You were miles away."

Sean smiled at his thoughts. "Just thinking about that call, darl..."

"Excuse me, Doctor Flynn, but what did you tell me about raking up the past?" Nell said indignantly.

"Ah well, that was different," Sean told her.

"What's different about it? It's the past and according to you, it serves no purpose in recalling what happened then," Nell insisted.

Joel and Sheralyn looked at each other and then at Nell. "Are we witnessing a domestic?" Joel asked cheekily.

"Not at all," Sean reassured him. "I'm remembering pleasant things. Your mum has been plagued with bad dreams of the past and I don't think that's healthy."

"No, it isn't healthy," Joel agreed. "Mum?" he enquired curiously.

Nell sighed. "I just think it's a sign I'm growing older and please note that I said older, not old. I have been looking back quite a lot recently, not because I want to remember the unpleasant things, but somehow my mind just keeps drifting back."

Sheralyn chirped in. "Looks like it runs in the family then," she said. "Joel was harking back to Bolton just a couple of days ago..."

"Sher!" Joel scolded.

"Oh yes?" Nell commented. "And what part of our Bolton life was that?" she asked, instantly wondering if Joel actually had any happy memories of life in Bolton.

Joel thought quickly. "I was wondering how Bolton Wanderers were going on," he quickly told the obviously concerned Nell. "They're in the Premier League now. I wish I could go to watch them, that's all." It was a lie and his wife knew it was.

Nell forced a smile. She knew her son well and she was aware that he'd thought on his feet in this instance. "Well, Bolton is a long way away and a long time ago," she said. "We are all very fortunate to be here and I thank my lucky stars every day."

"Do you mean this lucky star?" Joel asked pointedly tapping his chest.

~ * ~

...I'm Shane Obertelli. I work for the TV Network operating out of Melbourne, but we're setting up a station in Perth. We need a young, vibrant presenter for a talent show and you fit the bill perfectly, young man. What d'yer say?"

"I say what an offer!" Joel enthused. "How could I refuse that?"

Shane Obertelli was delighted. "It'll take a while to organise. You'll need an obligatory audition, but I guess in six months we'll be ready to go. We'll set the ball rolling as soon I'm back in Melbourne."

~ * ~

Collecting his thoughts again, Joel waited for his mother's response.

"Well," Nell replied, recognizing the arrogance in his enquiry. "I'll ignore your blatant conceit, young man," she continued, "I meant you, Sean and Sheralyn; possibly Sheralyn most of all because she took you off my hands and led you down the straight and narrow." Her quick retort wasn't lost on her son.

"Okay, I'm sorry, Mum. I don't know why I was thinking about Bolton. Something just triggered it, I guess," he said, his tone placatory. *It would only upset her if I told the truth, that I was thinking of her interfering in my life.* His wife read his mind and nodded in agreement.

Interrupting their discussion, Glenn called from the pool. "What time do we eat, Nan? I'm starving."

"You're always starving," Sheralyn called back. "Anybody would think I didn't feed my kids," she said to Nell and then she called to her children, "Come on, you three, isn't it time you came out of the water and dried off? Poppy will be getting the barbie going soon."

Sean thrilled at the title 'Poppy.' It was so Australian, so affectionate; so accepting of his role within his step-family. *I love it*, he thought. *I feel like their real grandfather and yet I don't think I'll ever feel like Joel's father. Nell planted too many memories of Tom in his mind as he was growing up and rightly so since he died before Joel got to know him, but I guess I come third in the father stakes. Joel's college tutor, Dafydd Powell, definitely showed Joel what a loving father should be like. He was there for him when he most needed a father. I just hope Joel sees me as a father-figure after all these years. I really do hope so. The main thing is that we think alike and that's good.*

Eight

For Kim, lunch near the Sydney Opera House was a new experience. Simon had deliberately chosen the harbour-side restaurant to impress his British visitor. "Considering this is your first trip to Australia," he said, "I thought I would show you what you have obviously only seen in pictures. Impressive or what?"

"Very impressive; fantastic even," she said, "I never thought I'd ever be sitting eating lunch overlooking Sydney Harbour with magnificent views of the famous bridge and the iconic Opera House, but actually it isn't my first visit to Australia."

"Oh, I understood you had never been here."

"I went to Perth when I was seven or eight years old. I was a bridesmaid for somebody I don't know. It was Christmas and I was very upset that Santa hadn't figured out where I was. Mum and Dad assured me that my presents would be at home in Bolton when we got back..." She stopped as her eyes glazed over.

"Are you all right, Kim?" Simon asked gently.

She looked at her lunch companion and noted for the first time how attractive he was. *Typical Italian stock,* she thought. *Tanned skin, dark eyes, excellent haircut…and tall, too. Probably early thirties.* "I'm fine," she told him, forcing herself to continue the conversation. "I don't remember anything about the trip at all and for some strange reason it has never been discussed at home, and I mean *never*. A couple of weeks ago, I got some sort of flashback about the wedding. It was very weird."

"Maybe it was because Australia triggered something in your subconscious," Simon offered.

"Might have been if I'd received your call before then, but it was my boyfriend talking about getting married and a wedding that actually made me remember."

Simon tried to hide his disappointment. "Oh, you're getting married?" he asked cheerily.

Kim coughed nervously. "Nope," she said pointedly.

"Subject closed?" he asked equally pointedly.

"Subject closed."

At two o'clock precisely, they arrived back at the office. Janine's friendly smile had returned, but Kim noticed her gaze fell on Simon and not on her.

"Any calls, Jan?" he asked breezily.

"One from the TV company, the new one, not urgent, but will you call back at your convenience? And your mother called to remind you about dinner."

"Fine, I'll call when I've sorted things with Kim. I don't want to be disturbed for an hour at least. Thanks, Jan."

The meeting went well. Simon explained that a pilot television show, *Performing for Australia,* had set the world of entertainment alight. "There were a lot of acts that could only be described as abysmal, but there were a few who really got agents clamouring at their doors. The TV company—the new one Janine mentioned—contacted OTA to give us first option."

"Wow! Very encouraging for you," Kim commented.

"More so for the artistes," Simon interjected. "Personally, I think we have three who might make it in the UK, or in the States. They'll need managing closely, but these are the ones we would like you to see." He handed her photographs and résumés of the artistes.

"Do you have a recording I can watch before I see them live?" she asked. "I won't make any decision from a recording, especially for vocalists. My priority is always that they have to be able to perform live without all the enhancements of recording studio technology."

"You're very wise, but many singers mime these days and generally speaking, they get away with it."

"My clients don't," she stated emphatically. "I need to present them to the public as the complete product, not as a manufactured copy. It's just the way Premier Plus and I work."

"I have two vocalist acts and an illusion act for you. The female vocalist is Eliza Marie; the other, a trio, goes under the name of Carousel. The group is made up of two girls and a guy. The illusionists are called Focus. They are a couple, married actually. There is a recording of the show I'll let you have before you leave the office. I've arranged for you to see them tomorrow at Studio Starlight. That's a rehearsal studio used by most of the TV channels in Sydney."

"Sounds great. I'll look forward to it," Kim said. "Are we all finished?"

"Not quite." Simon unexpectedly took her hand. It was not a handshake, but more a friendly gesture. "I am required to invite you out for dinner. My mother's call was to remind me of that. She would like you to meet us as a family and have a genuine Australian Italian dinner at our home." He grinned. "Mothers are priceless, aren't they?" He held on to her hand rather longer than necessary.

There was a knock on the door and Janine entered just as Kim was removing her hand from his grasp. The receptionist's eyes were drawn to their hands and her expression, Kim noticed, was one that could only be regarded as hostile. She glared at Simon who deliberately turned his back and walked towards the window.

Janine spoke with obvious irritation. "That was your father on the phone," she growled. "He will not be home for dinner as he has an important meeting with James Radicchio."

"Has somebody upset you, Janine?" Simon asked calmly, still looking out of the window on to the busy street below.

"Not that *you'd* notice," she replied with obvious sarcasm.

Kim was embarrassed. *It doesn't take a super brain to see there is some sort of history between these two.* "I'd better be off," she said.

Simon turned and moved towards her. "I'll pick you up at your hotel at six," he told her and taking hold of her hands again, he leaned forward and kissed her on each cheek.

Kim was taken aback. "Right, I'll see you then. Do I dress for dinner?" she asked.

"Casual is fine. Whatever you are comfortable in. See you later and thank you. Our meeting went well."

She walked past Janine whose body language was nothing less than threatening. Kim closed the door gently behind her. Pausing briefly to regain her composure, she couldn't help but hear Simon's voice. "Don't you ever do that again in front of a colleague, Janine, or you'll find yourself out of a job."

Kim left the building so as not to eavesdrop on a conversation that was really none of her business.

Back in Simon's office, the confrontation continued.

"You were all over her," Janine spat at him.

Simon looked directly at her. "Grow up, Janine. You have no right to pass judgment on my actions and for your information, I took her hand in a friendly gesture; I kissed her on the cheek as all Italians do when they leave a friend and..." He paused to choose his words carefully. "I have told you before that I took you out for dinner a couple of months ago as a thank you for dealing proficiently with the *Performing for Australia* paperwork. If you got the wrong idea, I'm sorry, but there will never be anything more than a working relationship between you and me. How many times do I have to explain that to you? That's just the way it is. Is that clear?

Janine stared at the floor and did not answer.

"Is that clear?" Simon repeated emphatically.

"If you say so," she mumbled and turned to leave the room so as not to allow him to see the anger in her eyes.

~ * ~

Dinner with the Obertellis was a very relaxed occasion. Kim was made to feel welcome immediately.

"I'm Mama Obertelli," Simon's mother said as she introduced herself. "My name is Rosalia, but please call me Mama O." She had not lost her accent in the fifty years she had been in Australia.

"Thank you. I'll be delighted to call you Mama O," Kim told her, "and thank you for inviting me to dinner in your home."

"To be a young girl on her own in Sydney is not ideal. You either eat in your hotel room, or go to restaurants you don't know. When my Simon told me you were coming to Sydney for the first time, I had to invite you."

"Now, now, Mama, don't embarrass the poor girl."

Kim smiled. "I'm not embarrassed. I'm very grateful I've been invited, and as your mother says, it's much more preferable to a lonely hotel room, or a restaurant I don't know. Either way, dining with you all is ten times better than eating alone."

"Only ten?" Simon joked.

"Maybe a few times more, but don't push your luck," she rejoined.

"Quick-witted too!" he said with a grin. "I like that."

When Lui and his wife, Marilena arrived, they sat down to typical Italian fare. Conversation was light and easy; there was much merriment and laughter, lots of talk about childhood pranks and family memories of growing up in Australia.

Kim briefly told them about growing up in a northern English town. "It was just a normal childhood...well what I would call normal. I was five when my brother was born so I was always the big, bossy sister."

"Bossy, hey?" Simon commented. "I'll have to remember that."

"Have you travelled much?" Lui asked. "We Aussies are intrepid travellers... that is, all except my brother!"

"I have travelled throughout Australia and New Zealand," Simon reminded his brother. "I just haven't got around to doing Europe yet. Dad never had time to take us and since I've been in the business, there has never been an appropriate time."

"They sound like excuses to me," Lui told him.

"Luigi, Luigi, leave your little brother alone," Mama O interjected. "He never wanted to leave his mama!"

Everybody laughed at that and Simon simply conceded with a conciliatory smile and shrugged.

"Well, I can suggest a remedy," Kim announced. "You must come to London and stay with me, Simon. I live on the river and I also have an apartment in Chelsea. When you've shown me how OTA operates, I'll return the compliment at Premier Plus."

Lui nudged his brother. "Now there's an offer you can't refuse, little bro. It isn't everyday a beautiful English rose invites you to stay with her!"

Simon thanked Kim and added, "We'll see. Maybe you can share some of your theatrical secrets with me." He was quiet after that and pondered on the possibilities of OTA and Premier Plus becoming a joint venture. *Not beyond the realms of possibility,* he thought.

Just as Simon prepared to drive Kim back to her hotel, Shane Obertelli arrived, apologising profusely for not being home for dinner.

"Hi, Papa," Simon greeted his beloved father. "This is Kimberley Mason from Premier Plus UK."

"Pleased to meet you, Mr. Obertelli. I believe you know my mentor, Theo Pendennis."

"Hello, young lady. How're you goin'? I can't claim to know Pendennis. I never met the guy, but we have done business with each other over the years." He peered over his glasses at Kim. "My God, you remind me of a young guy I introduced to Australian television well over twenty years ago. He had the same colouring as you—blond hair and brown eyes. It's unusual to find the two together naturally. He was English too. Joel Winston. He made it pretty big over here."

"I've never heard of him," Kim replied amicably.

"We have to go, Papa. We have a big day ahead tomorrow," Simon told his father.

"Okay, *figlio mio,* but allow some time for me too. I have some important business to discuss with you. I've been in a meeting with James Radicchio tonight. *Buona notte*, Kimberley. Hopefully I'll see you again before you leave Australia."

"I hope so," Kim replied. "Goodnight."

The half hour drive to the city was full of private thoughts for both Kimberley and Simon. He was thinking he liked the girl who was sitting by his side. *She's different; clever, completely in control; she's witty, good company and extremely polite.* His heart skipped a beat and he stole a glance to his left. He smiled when he caught her eye. *Slow down, Simon. You've just met her. You'll frighten her off if you give her any hint of your feelings. Feelings? Could it be possible I might be falling in love? Concentrate on your driving, idiot!*

Kim's mind was in turmoil with all manner of different thoughts. *What a day! First the meeting, not to mention Janine's mood swings. What on earth was that all about? Lunch by the harbour and the Opera House; fantastic. The recordings of the acts we're going to see tomorrow... pretty good, but I want to see them perform live. I have to keep an open mind. Dinner with the Obertellis, such lovely people. And Simon...* She looked to her right, just as he was looking at her. She smiled. He smiled. *Stop it, Kim! Concentrate on the job you have to do...*

They drew into the guests' car park at the Sydney Hilton. "I'll see you up to your room," Simon suggested. "I'll feel happier if I know you arrived home safely."

"Thanks, but there really is no need," Kim replied.

"Maybe I've seen too many movies, but all sorts of things can happen to a girl in underground car parks and in elevators," he explained with a grin. "Honestly, I'll be happy to see you to your room." He paused. "No ulterior motives, I assure you."

"Okay, if it makes you happy," she said as he got out of the Mercedes and walked round to open the door for her.

Kim elegantly swung her long legs out of the car as he offered his hand to help. He focused on the car's roof so as not to make it obvious that his heart was beating fast and he was inwardly gasping for breath. He gently placed his arm around her to guide her to the elevator.

"Have you got your room key?" he asked.

"In my bag," she said. "I'm always meticulous about what I need at any particular time. If you met my ex-boyfriend, he would tell you I'm obsessed."

"And are you?"

"Of course not. What's wrong with being organised?" She quickly dismissed all thoughts of Rick from her mind. *He's chosen to stay away from me; his loss.*

They arrived at her door, Room 392. She swiped the keycard in the lock and as the little green light flashed, she opened the door. Turning to face Simon, she smiled and said, "Thank you for bringing me home safely." She casually kissed him on the cheek.

Giving her an affectionate hug, he said, "My pleasure. I'll see you at the office at eight-thirty in the morning. Today has been very pleasant. *Buona notte,* Kimberley Mason."

"*Buona notte,* Simon Obertelli."

She watched him walk down the corridor to the elevator and then went inside. She threw her bag on the bed and kicked off her shoes before she entered the en suite to remove her make-up. She switched on the light…"Oh my God; what on earth…" Written on the mirror in bright red lipstick were the words, 'LEAVE HIM ALONE, OR ELSE!'

Nine

Simon was waiting for Kim when she arrived at his office the next morning. "G'day, Miss Mason. How are you today?"

"I'm good, thanks. Yourself?" Kim had a twinkle in her eye. "I'm getting the lingo off to a tee," she told him. "Are we ready to go?"

"Almost. Janine didn't come into work this morning, so I've had to call in our part-timer to cover."

Kim was impressed with the way he covered staff emergencies. "So you have a list of substitutes? Good going, Mr. Obertelli," she enthused. "Is Janine sick?"

"I don't know; she didn't answer her phone when I called," Simon replied. "It's not usual for her to stay away without calling in. In fact, it's not usual for her to be off work at all. I'll get Sarah to give her a call. We have to be at Studio Starlight at ten o'clock, so we'd better be off. We'll go down to Circular Quay and get a train. It will be quicker."

The journey took forty-five minutes. "Good public transport system," Kim commented. "Similar to the underground in London. Very reliable."

Simon was pensive.

"Hello-o? Are we with it today, or are we playing guess the answer?" Kim could see he was pre-occupied about something, but tried to lighten the mood.

"I'm bothered about Janine," he confided. "She's a funny girl at times; very efficient, but she has odd ways about her."

I've noticed, Kim thought. *Do I tell him about the mirror message or not? I can't be sure it was Janine who did it, but I could hazard a very good guess. Who else could it be?*

"Now you've gone quiet," he observed. "Is something bothering you?"

"I don't know if I should be worried or not and I'm not sure I ought to be telling you this..."

Simon sat up straight and looked at her questioningly. "What's wrong?" he asked.

Kim bit her bottom lip and breathed in deeply. "Well" she said slowly. "Last night, soon after you left, I found a message on my mirror written in red lipstick..."

"What sort of message? It's beginning to sound like a horror movie."

Kim had to smile at that. "Not quite," she assured him, "and I'm not easily scared, if that's what you are thinking, but it said 'Leave him alone, or else!' I knew there was some friction between you two because of the way she spoke to you as I left yesterday."

"You are joking!" he exclaimed. "I can't believe she would go to such lengths..."

"You are assuming it was her," Kim interjected. "How would she have known my room number and more to the point, how could she get in?"

"It's a mystery," he said thoughtfully, then, "Shit!" he exclaimed as the realisation hit him.

"Excuse me?"

"Sorry about the swearing, but I'm Australian and that's what we do sometimes." He grinned mischievously, but then almost as quickly as the grin had appeared, it disappeared. "Damn!" he said. "I asked her to book the room for you and get all the details in case I needed to contact you before our appointment."

"Okay, but it still doesn't explain how she would gain access to the room. Surely the hotel staff wouldn't have given her a key."

"I think *I* could find a way if I desperately wanted to. It wouldn't take much thinking out. Maids go in and out of the rooms all day as they go about their duties and they always turn down the beds in the evening," he said. "I think we're correct in assuming she's the culprit."

"Just give her the benefit of the doubt for the time being. She was so friendly towards me when I arrived," Kim told him.

"This is our stop," he said. "We'll have to discuss it later. You're sure you're okay?" Kim nodded confidently. "Now this is where our work together begins."

~ * ~

Kim treated the performances like auditions. The artistes were nervous and she was prepared to make allowances for nerves, but she asked if they might each do the performance for a second time so as to make sure she knew what she had to deal with. She silently evaluated each act. *Eliza Marie really hasn't improved on her first performance; Carousel, I think I can find work for them. They're good, and Focus is different. I don't think we have seen anything like them before in the UK. I'm sure I could interest the television companies and probably clubs all over the country.* When all three acts had shown her much of their repertoire, she was ready to see them individually, but with Simon there to take care of their interests.

"I think you need to work on your live performance," she told the disappointed Eliza Marie. "This is not to say you haven't got what it takes, but I'd like to come back to see you in about a year."

"Are you just being diplomatic?" Simon asked her when Eliza Marie had left the room.

"Of course not!" she insisted. "I don't work like that. She has a good voice that needs developing for live performances. If I put her through the British club scene, she'd fall at the first hurdle. The punters are very discerning and want the polished article. I think she needs more time to develop."

"Shall we bring in Carousel? Are they going to receive the brush-off, too?"

Kim's hackles were rising. "Look, Simon, you invited me here to assess these acts and that's what I'm doing. If you object to my decisions, then OTA and Premier Plus have no future together..."

"I wasn't objecting. I want what is right for my clients. I thought Eliza Marie could improve on the job as it were," he said adamantly.

"In that case, you put her out in Australia and see what happens. You'll be sending a lamb to the slaughter in my opinion, but that's exactly what it is—my opinion. You either accept it, or you don't. At the moment, I'm not prepared to take the responsibility for her."

"Tell it like it is, won't you, Kim?" Simon sounded serious, but she detected a twinkle in his dark eyes. *This girl is very forthright,* he thought. *Confident to the extreme.*

"If you want pussy-footing, you'll not get it from me, Mr. Obertelli. You know as well as I do that this is a cut-throat business. Why tell them they're good just because it's what they want to hear?" She paused, not for effect, but to collect her thoughts. "Now we'll bring in Carousel."

~ * ~

Back in the office the following day, the atmosphere was brighter. "I'm pleased you're taking on Carousel and Focus," Simon told her for the umpteenth time.

"I know you're pleased," she replied. "What did you expect? Come on, Simon, you know when an act has that special *je ne sais quoi*. I'm happy to look after both acts when they arrive in the UK. The timing is important. I suggest they come over in March, just after Easter. I'll work on my contacts in preparation for the summer season in the UK. Theatres in holiday resorts put on a lot of shows during the holiday season and I also deal with European resorts, Spain and Greece in particular. The acts get to travel to the hot spots in Europe. Some of the venues are in five-star luxury hotels. What could be better grounding than that?"

"Sounds good to me."

"I'm also working on a contract with cruise companies, so who knows, they might go down well on the cruise ships, if you'll pardon the expression." She grinned. "Bad turn of phrase in that context," she admitted.

"Rather," he agreed.

"Now that's settled, we'll complete the paperwork, draw up contracts and then I'll be on my way. I'm going to go to Perth tomorrow for a couple of days." She stood and walked towards the door. "Now, I must use the little girls' room," she said. "Excuse me for a moment, please."

Kim found the ladies' room and as she passed the reception desk, she nodded to Janine who had returned to work after her reported migraine attack. Since the mirror fiasco a couple of days previously, the two women had not set eyes on each other. When Kim returned from freshening up, she looked directly at Janine and stopped in her tracks.

"Do you like this colour?" Janine asked as she produced a bright red lipstick. She took out a handbag mirror and proceeded to daub the lipstick around her mouth very precisely and very thick. She pouted sensuously and blew a contemptuous kiss towards Kim. "Lovely, isn't it?" Her expression was verging on the offensive.

"What on earth are you doing?" Kim asked.

"Just showing you how serious I am about..."

The office door opened and Simon called out. "Are you ready, Kim? We have work to do."

Janine grabbed a tissue and swiftly removed the lipstick from her mouth without turning to face her employer. "His majesty needs you," she hissed through clenched teeth.

"Indeed he does," Kim replied cheerily. "Isn't it wonderful to be needed?"

Back in the office, Simon looked bemused. "What was all that about?"

"Oh, I think we have just confirmed who delivered the mirror message," she said unconcerned. "That girl has problems and *I'm* not going to be the one to sort them out. Your department, Mr. Obertelli."

"Oh bugger! I'd forgotten about that. I'm so sorry, Kim. That was really remiss of me."

Kim smiled, a very friendly, *I understand* smile. "Not a problem, for me anyway. Once I leave the office today, she won't feel threatened, I'm sure, but you might! Now let's get to work."

With the details sorted, Kim stood up to leave when the telephone rang. Simon picked up the phone. "Simon Obertelli..."

Kim gestured that she was leaving and mouthed that she would meet Simon for dinner as it was her last night in Sydney. "Seven o'clock," she whispered, "at the Hilton."

Simon nodded, smiled and waved goodbye.

~ * ~

Dinner was delightful. "Good food, good wine and good company," Simon commented. "Thank you for inviting me."

"It's the least I could do. You have been very kind and very welcoming and I'm grateful for that," Kim told him. "You have made my first trip to Sydney very enjoyable."

They wandered into the residents' bar and ordered coffee and liqueurs. Finding a sofa in an alcove by a window that overlooked the city, they settled down to relax and leave all the work conversation behind. "Tell me about this boyfriend of yours," Simon suggested.

"Why do you want to know about him? And anyway, we broke up a few weeks before I came out here," she divulged.

"Would it be rude of me to ask why?" Simon continued. "I'm just curious and I want to get to know you better."

"What do you want to know?" she asked. "I don't think I need tell you about Rick if it's me you are interested in."

"Who said I was interested in you?" he quipped. "I said I wanted to get to know you. If we're going to form a working relationship..."

"Work talk is taboo tonight," she retorted.

"I know that, but if I know why you broke up with him, it'll help me to know what annoys you!" He looked directly at her and smiled. *Stop beating around the bush, idiot. You are flirting outrageously and she knows it.*

"Okay," she conceded, "The honest answer is I didn't love him. We'd been together five years and I was still regarding him as a friend, a very close friend if you get my meaning, but I couldn't see myself spending the rest of my life with him."

"Did you live together?"

"No. That was part of the problem. He wanted to move in with me; I just wanted the weekend arrangement that worked for me, but not for him. He couldn't understand that I need something more from my life, not just the husband, wife and kids thing."

"Something more?" Simon asked. "You're confusing me now, Kim, and I'm usually a pretty good judge of character. What more can there be to beginning a happy family life together?"

Kim laughed. "I confuse myself at times and I must confess, sometimes I really don't know what I want myself," she joked. "Seriously though, I have this strange feeling there's something missing from my life and I don't know what it is."

"Maybe it's that certain *je ne sais quoi* we look for in our clients," Simon suggested light-heartedly.

"Perhaps, but you know, it's a very weird feeling. If I were into all that psychic stuff, I'd go to a clairvoyant, the instinct is so strong," she revealed. "Actually, I feel a peculiar sense of relief just talking to you about it. Rick always pooh-poohed the idea. He thought I was using it as an excuse not to get married."

"And were you?"

Kim thought for a moment. *Was I using it as an excuse, or was it just convenient to stop Rick going on about the marriage thing?* She cocked her head to one side, looking very young and vulnerable.

"My, my, Miss Mason, how coy is that expression?" Simon remarked with an appreciative smile. *So she has got a sensitive side after all.*

She felt her cheeks burning. She lowered her gaze as she smiled uncharacteristically shyly and said, "I didn't mean it to be. I was simply trying to choose my words carefully." She reached out and touched his arm, a slightly more than friendly gesture. "I suppose it *was* an excuse really to stop Rick asking me to marry him for the umpteenth time. The real reason was, as I told you earlier, I didn't love him. I hadn't worked out how to break it gently to him at the time. As it actually happened, he took the huff and walked out anyway, but not before telling me I'd end up a lonely, frustrated, old maid."

"Ouch!" Simon voiced with feeling. "I sense he was none too pleased."

"He didn't contact me for weeks after that, so eventually I called him and said I presumed it was over. He simply said 'Yes it is.' He had always said he wouldn't give up on me, but he did in the end. He obviously wasn't as heart-broken as I had thought he would be—arrogance on my part perhaps—but he was seen in Stringfellow's a week later, draped around a very attractive and attentive girl, and here I am." She smiled amicably. "I have no regrets. Life goes on and all that. Anyway, what about you?"

Simon shrugged. "No serious relationships; just casual dates. I once went out with a girl for three months until she dumped me for a younger man," he said with the familiar twinkle in his eye. "To be honest, I haven't met anybody yet who I have fallen in love with. I have *liked* my girlfriends, but never experienced love, whatever love might be." *I'd like to tell you that I've fallen head over heels in love with you, Kimberley Mason, but I'm afraid I might get my heart broken.* "I'm going to be thirty-two years old next birthday so I guess I ought to be looking more seriously for a life partner."

"I know somebody not a million miles away who'd jump at the chance..."

Simon's heart missed a beat. *Is she propositioning me?* He looked at her with raised eyebrows.

"Janine!"

"You have to be joking!" he exclaimed.

"Well, she's made it pretty clear to me she has the hots for you! What's the story behind all that? I think I have the right to ask," she told him pointedly.

"Indeed you have," he agreed. "She is an excellent receptionist *cum* PA. When *Performing for Australia* took off, she did a wonderful job in dealing with the organisation and the completion of the paperwork. I took her out to dinner as a thank you for all her hard work." He took a deep breath before he continued. "When I dropped her off at home afterwards, she came on pretty strong to me and I had to tell her I wasn't interested."

Kim looked at the man sitting beside her who appeared decidedly uncomfortable relating what had happened. "Was it really that bad? An attractive girl giving you the come-on should be very flattering," she told him gently to reassure him.

"She leaned over to me in the car and kissed me, a full on the lips kiss and..."

"And what?" Kim asked as she took his hand in hers.

Simon smiled, not at what he was about to say, but at Kim who was making him feel more at ease. "She took my hand and placed it on her breast..."

Kim waited in silence.

"... and then she grabbed my crotch..."

Kim had to stifle a giggle.

"...I pushed her away, got out of the car and went round to open the passenger door to let her out. That's it! Nothing more, nothing less. However, she and I haven't spoken about what happened since then, other than when she reacted to you being with me in the office."

"Maybe she thinks not saying anything means you didn't mind," Kim suggested. She was still holding on to his hand and it seemed the natural thing to do.

"She can be under no illusions now, because after you left this afternoon, I gave her notice to leave OTA."

"How can you be so sure she won't retaliate in some way?" Kim asked. "She's pretty intense about things."

Simon gently squeezed her hand. "She needs a reference and as an act of good faith, I suggested she apply to the new TV channel that's emerging. I told her I would contact James Radicchio who is the managing director to say how proficient she is, but it comes with the proviso that she does nothing more to blot her copybook. I told her I knew about the lipstick too."

"Wow! What did she say about that?"

"Not a lot when I made it very clear to her I would inform the police if she ever did or said anything to make you feel uncomfortable in any way, shape, or form," he said. "She's not a bad person. She thinks I've rejected her and we all know that hell hath no fury like a woman scorned."

"A bit clichéd, but thank you for that," and she leaned forward to kiss him on the cheek.

"Kim?"

"Yes?"

"I like you. Please don't go away and never come back."

She moved closer to him and whispered in his ear. "I like you too..." They stood slowly and wandered towards the elevator to go to her room.

Ten

Simon had breakfast with Kim at the Hilton and then drove her to the airport. "Thank you for last night," he whispered as he kissed her goodbye.

"Please don't thank me," Kim chastised. "We made love and I want to know that's exactly what it was–L-O-V-E. Saying thank you makes me feel like a call girl!" She grinned impishly.

Simon picked her up and swung her around as she looked lovingly into his dark eyes. Placing her gently back on her feet, he cupped her face in his hands and looked at her affectionately. "You know," he said, "Dad was right. It is rare to find brown eyes and naturally blonde hair together. You are quite stunning, Miss Mason, and I adore you."

"But not unique, apparently. What was the name of the guy your dad knew?"

"Joel Winston. I remember watching his show when I was a kid. It was a talent show rather like *Performing for Australia*. He was a good singer, too; a brilliant all-round performer. We are hoping he'll take over the Perth branch of OTA when we get it off the ground. Maybe you'll get to meet him soon."

Kim regarded the new love in her life with questioning eyes. "I go back to London soon. I have work to do, don't forget," she reminded him. "I can't leave Melissa in charge for too long. Melissa's my PA. She's very reliable and good at what she does, but she isn't me and I like to be completely in charge at Premier Plus—my agency, my way." She said the words and shivered.

"Okay, Miss Independent, I get the picture, but why are you shivering?"

Simon held her close. "Somebody walked over my grave," she said and then admitted, "I had the weirdest feeling then as I said those words–*my agency, my way*. A very weird *déjà vu* sensation, but I don't recall ever using them previously, not in that context anyway."

"Don't worry, darl, I'm here to protect you," he reassured her. "And that's the boarding call for the Perth flight. Call me when you land and remember..."

"I love you too," she pre-empted him. "I'll come back to Sydney before I leave for the UK. Promise."

~ * ~

Perth was an awe-inspiring place for her. She hired a car and spent three days sight-seeing. The most impressive area for her was King's Park, a vast area of parkland overlooking the Swan River and the city. She stood and surveyed the landscape. *This is so strange,* she thought. *I feel like I belong here and yet I don't think I've been here before.*

~ * ~

1971. *Joel hired a car and drove to Perth. His discovery of King's Park, an enormous, absolutely beautiful area of scenic parkland in the middle of the metropolis, overlooking the Swan*

River and the city of Perth, filled him with awe. There were driveways, walkways, cycle paths, magnificent views over the city and what he noticed more than anything, it was so clean and litter free. King's Park had a magical aura about it and in an instant, he knew he would indeed be back to settle in Western Australia. He already felt like he belonged...

~ * ~

Kim thought she'd better call home. She had not spoken to her parents since she arrived in Australia. "I'm in Perth," she told her father. "It's an absolutely beautiful city."

"But I thought you were going to Sydney," Ben said, unsure of how to react to her news for fear of upsetting Belinda.

"I've been to Sydney. I had just over a week there and met some most fantastic people." *Better not mention Simon just yet.* "I have signed up two acts and I'm bringing them over to London after Easter. The agency I'm working with had previous dealings with Theodore Pendennis—can you believe that? Apparently, Shane Obertelli, the agency's founder, did business with Theo on numerous occasions, but they never met. Incredible, or what?"

"Small world, hey?" Ben said cheerily. "When will you be home?"

"I don't know yet. I would like to go to Melbourne just to suss out possible links there and I am definitely going back to Sydney before I leave for the UK," she informed her father.

"Why do you need to go back to Sydney?"

"I met an amazing family who I want to spend time with before I go home."

"Do you mean they have an amazing son?" Ben asked. "I know you too well, Kimberley Mason."

"Dad!" she cried. "Why do you have to be so..." She paused to find the right word.

"So astute?" he offered.

"How come I got to have such an awesome dad?" she asked. "Love you, Daddy!"

"Love you too, sweetheart."

"Is Mum there?"

"Not at the moment. She's out with Auntie Penny. Pen has come over to Bolton for a few days break and some girlie catch up time with your mum," Ben told her.

"That's a shame—that she's not there, I mean. I know she'll have a great time with Auntie Penny, but tell her I called, won't you?"

"Of course I will. Now you take care and don't speak to any strangers," he instructed.

"Okay, Daddy. It's a long time since you needed to say that to me when I was going out, but I'm a big girl now," she reminded him.

"I know, baby, more's the pity. I really miss my little Kimberley sometimes," Ben said wistfully.

"Oh Dad, you know I'll always be your little girl," she reassured him.

"Yes, sweetheart, I do know that. You'll always be daddy's little princess."

"Oh, by the way, have you ever heard of anyone called Joel Winston?"

Ben took a sharp intake of breath. *Hell's teeth,* he thought, *how do I deal with this?* "Somebody with that name went to the same school as I did," he said quickly.

"Oh well, apparently he made it big over here. Don't know much about him, but Shane Obertelli says he and I have the same colouring, brown eyes and blonde hair..."

"Is that so?" Ben asked in an attempt to cover the turmoil he was feeling inside.

"And I thought I was unique!" she joked.

"And so you are, baby. You are very unique," he told her, "and don't you ever forget it."

~ * ~

Belinda and Penny arrived home from shopping just as Ben replaced the receiver. "Oh, you've just missed Kim," he told them. "She seems to be having a whale of a time."

"Did you get a number so we can call back?" Belinda asked.

"No, I didn't, but I'm sure she'll call again soon." Ben was dismissive and Belinda noticed.

"Ben?" she asked pointedly.

"She's in Perth," he conceded. "I didn't want to tell you."

"Oh bloody hell!" Belinda said as she grabbed hold of Penny's arm.

Penny stood by as Ben told Belinda about Kim's call. "Look, Bel," she said gently. "Kim doesn't know anything about Joel, does she, let alone about his being in Perth? How on earth can she bump into somebody she doesn't know?"

Belinda looked anxious. "I have all these imagined situations in my head that won't go away," she revealed. "You know as well as I do that she's the image of Joel. What if they are in a shopping mall and walk past each other and do a double take? What if they are in the same restaurant? What if they..."

"What if? What if? What if?" Ben snapped. "Damn it, Bel, use your common sense. For thirty years we have never uttered Joel's name in front of Kim. We have to trust we have done what we felt was right for us and for Kim." His mind was spinning. *I daren't tell Belinda that Joel's name cropped up during that phone call. She would go demented. Hopefully, I was dismissive enough to put Kim off finding out more about him.* He felt the need to reiterate what had been said many times before. "When we were over there for the wedding, we only referred to Joel as Daddy's friend and her uncle. We didn't say his name directly to her and immediately after the wedding, we were off on our travels so as to make the most of our once in a lifetime trip. She was too young to fully understand what was going on; thrilled to dress up to be a bridesmaid, but she was watching the boats on the river while the wedding speeches were going on and more concerned that Santa wouldn't know where to leave her presents. We even left her bridesmaid's dress behind. Think about it, Bel. She has no reason to think it was anything other than a holiday where she got to be a bridesmaid. She couldn't have cared less who was getting married."

"The whole situation worries me to death and before you castigate me further, I know I have to deal with it. I just can't get the disturbing thoughts out of my head, but as you say, what are the odds of Kim just bumping into Joel?" Her anxiety was obvious, but she continued, "Any more news?"

Ben related Kim's proposed visit to Melbourne and then her return to Sydney.

"Why is she going back to Sydney?" Belinda asked, "Is her work not finished there? I have to say, though, I'm more than relieved she won't be in Perth long enough for anything untoward to happen."

"I think she's met somebody," Ben told the two women whose jaws dropped simultaneously.

Penny was the first to speak. "Good on her!" she said. "I knew she wouldn't be single for long."

Belinda was more reserved in her comments. "How on earth can she carry on a relationship if he lives half a world away? Maybe it's just a holiday romance."

"She says she met a wonderful family. That's all I know. I just picked up on the son thing and she didn't deny it, but then again, she didn't confirm it either," Ben explained. "You know, we really have to allow her the space to lead her own life, for better or worse. She isn't a child anymore and she wouldn't thank us for interfering," but he simply couldn't stop the thought from entering his mind: *In that respect, she certainly is her father's daughter.*

~ * ~

After a week in Perth, Kim flew to Melbourne and called in the OTA office to introduce herself to the manager there. She learned that there were wonderful opportunities in the theatre world of Melbourne and felt that somewhere along the line, she would be able to work on the artiste exchange programme she planned to initiate when she returned to the UK. *I'll talk to Simon about it before I leave…God, I miss him. How on earth will I survive when we are ten thousand miles apart?*

She returned to Sydney knowing that in three day's time she needed to be on a plane back to London. Simon was waiting at the airport when she landed.

"I've missed you so much," he told her as he took her into his arms and held her as though he never wanted to let go.

"I've missed you too," she replied. "This situation wasn't supposed to happen, was it?"

"It wasn't planned, if that's what you are saying, but none of us has any say in what Fate throws our way. I firmly believe this was meant to be," he stated with confidence.

"But we live at opposite ends of the earth, Simon. How can we make it work with so much distance between us?" she asked plaintively.

"We'll make it work," he reassured her. "We have to. I love you, Kimberley Mason. I never felt like this and now that I have discovered what love is, I have no intention of letting it go."

"I love you too, Simon Obertelli." She grinned mischievously. "Thank goodness I reserved my room at the Hilton. Now we have something to confirm."

Equally mischievously, he replied, "Confirm? I think the word is consummate!"

Eleven

Kim returned to London in February to the harsh reality of British winter weather. Four weeks of the Australian summer became a distant memory as soon as she set foot on British soil where snow was falling and winds blew through her body like icy spears to chill the marrow in her bones. Melissa picked her up at the airport and drove her straight to the office where she needed to set the ball rolling for Carousel and Focus.

"Welcome back, Kim. I've missed you," Melissa said as they hurried through Heathrow's Terminal Four to the car park.

"Why do car parks have to be miles away from Arrivals? I hate airports! I wandered around Sydney airport for ages because I was dropped off at the Domestic Terminal instead of the International. Flippin' taxi drivers! As it happened, I had loads of time to spare before check in, so I had a coffee and bought a book, then I caught the shuttle across to where I was supposed to be. God, it's freezing," Kim groaned, "and I'm knackered! I really need my bed right now, but I have to start the negotiations for these two Australian acts as soon as possible."

"Can't it wait until tomorrow, Kim?" Melissa asked. "Surely you'll work better when you've had some sleep."

"I promised OTA I would get started immediately. I don't want to let them down," Kim stated. "It's February twenty-second now and I need to have them in situ after Easter. That gives me five weeks to contact the travel companies' entertainment managers so that they are able to sort out their programmes and organise the travel documents for the artistes."

"Leave the details with me, Kim and for goodness sake, go home and get some sleep. EtoS-travel and Atholympic Tours always give you carte blanche to provide the artistes you feel are most suited to their needs. Why is it all so urgent?"

"This is not just Premier Plus, Mel. It's OTA too and I have a responsibility to them as well as to myself." Kim was unusually stressed. "How far did you get with Pacific Cruise Ships while I was away?"

"Slow down, for goodness sake. You've just landed after a marathon flight. Pacific Cruise Ships can wait. This just isn't like you, Kim. What's wrong?" Melissa asked. She looked directly into Kim's eyes, eyes that showed strain and desperation she had never noticed before.

Kim looked at her colleague and friend. "I'm tired; I'm jet lagged and…" then hot tears coursed down her flushed cheeks.

"What on earth is the matter, Kim? I have never seen you like this," Melissa said.

Kim sniffed and wiped away the tears with the back of her hand. "I fell in love, Mel, and I want to be with him so much."

~ * ~

After two weeks of relaxing and family fun on the Gold Coast, Joel Winston and his family returned to their riverside home in South Perth. "I always enjoy being with Mum and Sean," he told

Sheralyn as they settled back to endure the five hour flight from Sydney back to WA, "but I'll be glad to be home. Why we couldn't fly direct from Coolangatta to Perth, I don't know, but that would be too easy, wouldn't it? Changing at Sydney is a real pain. Sometimes I think airlines just want to make a journey as difficult as possible," he grumbled.

"Who rattled your cage this morning?" Sheralyn asked. "We have always flown this way and you've never complained before. Just read your magazine from cover to cover and we'll be there in no time at all. Maybe you should buy yourself an electronic game like the kids have. Look at them...eyes down and fingers going fifteen to the dozen." She laughed. "I bet we won't hear a peep out of any of them for the next four hours."

Joel rested his head on the back of his seat. He closed his eyes to see if he might recall the image of the girl he'd just seen leaving the book shop. His thoughts were confused. *I shivered–I literally shivered. She had my hair (longer, of course) and dark eyes like mine.* He inwardly shivered again. *And I thought I was unique. I wonder what the odds are of meeting your double face-to-face. They say we all have at least one double somewhere in the world.*

"Penny for them, darl," his wife said, interrupting his reverie.

"Just thinking about what I have to do when we arrive home," he fibbed. "I'll have to contact Shane Obertelli sometime this week to tell him I've decided to take the job. Gosh, it must be almost thirty years since I've seen him."

~ * ~

In Bolton, England, Belinda Mason waited anxiously for her daughter to call when she arrived home. "The past few weeks have been hell," she told her husband on the morning she knew Kim landed back in London. "I think I'll call her when you've gone to work."

"Leave it a while, love. She's bound to be tired and if you question her too much about where she's been and who she met, she won't be pleased," he said. "You know how she reacts when she thinks we're interfering."

Just like her father, Belinda thought. "I have always tried not to interfere, Ben. You know that, but I'm her mother and I'm allowed to give my opinion. It's just that this trip of hers has opened up a lot of old wounds."

"Please, Bel, not again. We've gone over this so many times," Ben reminded her.

Belinda sighed. "Okay, I'll leave it until she calls us. I'm going into the salon this morning anyway. Samantha's got a doctor's appointment so I'm taking over her clients. I guess this will be a regular occurrence now that she's having a baby."

Ben smiled at the woman he had loved from the first time he saw her, even though her face was tear-stained then and she was in a mad rush to get away from the situation at the Connollys' shop. He recalled vividly the time he told Joel Winston what he thought of him…

…Ben returned after work with a very serious look on his face. "I've been with Belinda for the past few days …"

"Good one, Ben. I'm happy for you. I knew you'd get off with her."

"Shut up and listen, Joel," Ben continued. "I haven't slept with her, if that's what you're implying, but you did, didn't you?"

"Is that what she told you? Ben, it wasn't like you think…"

"Exactly what do I think, Joel? I'll tell you not what I think, but what I know. Belinda was in love with you, maybe still is. She didn't turn up for the gig because she was sick that morning and has been sick every morning since then. Get the picture, buddy?" Ben was seething.

Joel paled. "Shit! Oh shit!"

"Is that all you can say? How about, how is she now? How about, I must go to see her? How about, I'll stand by her?" Ben raged.

"But my career..." Joel cried. "What a mess!"
"You selfish bastard, Winston and I thought you'd changed.
From now on, you just keep away from Belinda. Do you hear
me? Keep well away." With that, Ben stormed out...

~ * ~

"What are you thinking about?" Belinda asked him.

"Honestly?" he asked.

"Of course, honestly," Belinda replied. "When haven't you been honest with me?"

*Just recently when Kim asked about Joel; if you knew...*he didn't want to imagine how she might react if he told her the whole truth this time. "I always try to be honest, you know that," he told her. "I was thinking about when I first met you, how I loved you at first sight even though you were crying and you rushed past me."

Belinda went to give him a hug, a long, affectionate embrace. "Sorry, darling. I've been a bit of a pain these last few weeks and I've obviously made you root up the past too. I hope you can forgive me. I do love you and I always will."

"I hope you do, and there's nothing to forgive. Now I have to go to work."

Tony, their son, popped his head round the door. "I'm off, you two lovebirds. Put her down, Dad. You don't know where she's been!" he quipped, unaware that his joke might be construed as extremely bad taste. "I'll be late home tonight, Mum. I have a staff meeting and then I'm meeting Liz to go and look at The Georgian House. She thinks that's where we'll have the reception. We'll grab a bite to eat in town."

"That's okay, love," Belinda said, "and not so much of your cheek. Your dad knows exactly where I've been!"

Ben smiled at her, a well done, well-handled and proud to be your husband smile.

~ * ~

In Queensland, Sean and Nell Quinn had waved off their family and returned to their Coomera River home. "I love having the family here," she said, "but I'm so exhausted when they leave. No matter how much you love your kids, it's still a strain to have them under the same roof twenty-four hours a day, seven days a week. I never seem to relax."

"Darl, you never relax when you're around Joel. You spoil him rotten!" Sean told her pointedly. "And it seems to me that it's just accepted by them all that Nana will wait on them hand and foot. You have to slow down, Nell, as you grow older."

Nell regarded her husband with a look of resignation in her eyes. "I know that, sweetheart, but I can't help thinking how Joel was my whole life all those years ago and yet, I think I would still have insisted he did everything my way even if I hadn't lost Tom when I did. That's the way I was at that time. This is a clear case of self-assessment and I can't say I like it. Do you think all these flashbacks I'm having could be my conscience rearing its ugly head?"

Sean took her hand and led her to the deck overlooking the river. The air was warm and soothing, the water calm and peaceful. "Darling Nell," he said quietly. "You have to let go of the past. You can't keep tying yourself up in knots over something you can't change. You'll drive yourself mad!"

"I know that, but I think I've worked out what it is that's bothering me...the missing bit of my dreams," she informed him.

"You have? Well, that's wonderful. Tell me so we can solve the problem together."

...He left his dalliance with Belinda until last.

"I didn't love her. We just got carried away on the wave of excitement, but she liked me and I didn't feel inclined to reciprocate, if you know what I mean..."

"Oh Joel," Nell whispered, "I did so try to get you to treat girls nicely."

"But I didn't treat her badly other than rejecting her..." he paused ominously, "and how many times had I been dumped? It didn't seem like a big deal to me at the time. I was honest with her about how I felt."

"So why is it bothering you now? Have you realised that you love her after all?" Nell asked, trying to make sense of the situation.

"She got pregnant."

"Oh my God!" Nell cried. "You're a father?"

"Well, yes and no," he confessed. "I got her pregnant, but Ben's the father."

Nell was confused. "I don't understand. You fathered a child, but Ben's the father? It doesn't make sense."

"Ben loved Belinda all along and he picked up the pieces when I did a runner. He told me to stay out of their lives and he put his name on the birth certificate." It sounded futile now, but it was nonetheless the truth.

"And now you would like to claim your child? Oh Joel, what a bloody mess!" Nell declared.

"No, I don't want to claim the child; I never did and Ben is the perfect father. We made our peace when he came to view the house," Joel told her.

"But..."

"I know what you're going to say, why did I talk about it when I was high? Well, I don't know. I guess it was in my subconscious. I really don't want to disrupt the child's life nine years on, nor would I ever come between Ben and Belinda. I still feel comfortable with the decision I made."...

"I have a grandchild I don't know..." Nell said with a frustrated sigh.

"Oh Nell, not that again! You met her at the wedding and she must be almost thirty years old by now, probably married with children of her own." Sean was aghast.

"In that case, I might be a great-grandmother and missing out on my great-grandchildren," she said sadly. "Do you think it would be irresponsible if I wrote to Ben and Belinda to ask how they are?"

"Indeed I do!" Sean exclaimed. "Nell, where is your common sense? They haven't contacted us for twenty years apart from the thank you card they sent after the wedding. We spent very little time with them because we were off on honeymoon and they travelled to Alice Springs the following day and then on to the Sunshine Coast to complete their holiday. If they wanted to keep in touch, they would have done so. Think about it, Nell. Ben is officially Kimberley's father and for all we know, the girl is completely unaware that he isn't who she thinks he is..."

Nell interrupted him. "I know all that, darl, and it was really Joel and Sheralyn's wedding they came to, not ours, even though it was a double wedding. I understand they would necessarily have left Joel and Sheralyn on their own to enjoy their honeymoon, but don't you think it odd they didn't catch up with Joel for a little while after the reception?"

Sean looked pointedly at his wife. "Nell, leave it, will you? We have no idea at all how they handled the Kimberley situation. On the surface, it all looks clear cut, but who's to say what really went on in their minds twenty years ago? My advice is to leave well enough alone. It really is none of our business."

Nell sighed. "I know you're right, babe, but I still feel there's something missing from my life and Kimberley is definitely the missing piece of the jigsaw."

"Promise me, Nell Flynn, that you won't do anything reckless and irresponsible as far as Kimberley Mason is concerned," he demanded.

Nell looked directly into her husband's questioning eyes and reluctantly nodded slowly.

Twelve

"I should have taken you to the airport myself," Simon told her when they spoke on the phone. "At least I'd have dropped you at the right terminal. Taxi drivers should know better. Maybe he'd had a row with his wife that morning and was preoccupied."

"I don't know, but I didn't realise myself until I went to look for my flight on the screen. It would have been nice for you to take me, but your meeting with James Radicchio was more important for you," Kim replied. "How did that go, by the way?"

"I'll tell you about that later. What's more important now is that I tell you how much I love you and miss you. We simply have to find some way of seeing each other again and soon," he said while his heart performed somersaults in his chest. "You have no idea what you have done to me, Miss Mason."

"I think I have, because I feel the same way," she said and she took a deep breath in an effort to stop the trembling she felt inside.

"I'm just about to go home from the office when I've finished talking to you. It's seven o'clock in the evening here and I know you are only just getting out of bed…" He paused. "I wish I could be there with you. I can see you now with your hair tousled and your dark eyes shining even when you have just wakened up. Oh Kim, I love you so much."

"I love you too, darling, and it's oh so wonderful. I don't know how we'll survive on daily phone calls, but we both have jobs to do and unless you can take time off to fly out here, I can't foresee when I'll be able to take another trip to Australia any time in the immediate future. Summer season is always busy for me." Kim tried to hide the desperation in her voice.

"Oh dear," Simon declared.

"What's wrong?" Kim asked. "That sounds ominous. Do I need to be worried?"

"No, but listen; James Radicchio would like to meet you…well, more than meet you," he revealed. "He wants you to come and be a guest judge on *Performing for Australia*. He's offered an all-expenses-paid trip for you to come out to do three live episodes. Do you think you could do it, Kim?"

"But I've never done television in my life, Simon!" she exclaimed. "How on earth did he come up with that idea?"

Simon coughed guiltily and Kim picked up that guilt ten thousand miles away on the other end of the phone. "What have you done?" she asked pointedly.

"W-e-l-l," he replied slowly, "I simply told him what a brilliant judge of talent you are, how beautiful you are, how honest you are, how…"

"Hey, hold on there," she interjected. "That's a very biased opinion and you know it."

"Now you're being modest and that's another of your endearing qualities," he said with a little laugh so she would know he was smiling.

Kim was almost lost for words. "I don't know what to say."

"That must be a first," he quipped.

Kim thought for a moment and then said, "Let me think about it, Simon. When would he want me?"

"Does that mean you'll come?" he asked excitedly.

"No, it doesn't, not yet anyway, but please answer the question. How soon would he want me?"

"He didn't give any dates, but the next series begins at the end of May. Perhaps I can ask him to include you in the latter part of the audition section. If you do a good job, he's bound to want you back for the final." Simon seemed to have it all planned.

"I need dates, Simon. This is business now, not a social visit. Then there's the little consideration of my fee," she said in her most business-like manner.

"Okay, babe, I'll get on to it tomorrow. In the meantime, remember I love you with all my heart and soul. The mere thought of you being here again just makes my day. I'll call tomorrow at the same time. Have a good day, darl. Don't work too hard. I'll be thinking of you," he told her and he blew kisses into the phone. "*Ciao*, sweetheart. Love you."

"*Ciao*, baby. Love you too."

In the office she informed Melissa of the offer of television work. "That's great, Kim; just fantastic," Melissa enthused. "You've got to take them up on it. It'll be wonderful exposure for Premier Plus, and you'll be able to see Simon again sooner than you expected. That's got to be a bonus!"

Kim was confused. "I'm not so sure, Mel," she reasoned. "Oh, I want to see Simon, that goes without saying, but that really isn't the issue here. Television appearances? Way out of my comfort zone."

~ * ~

"About time you called home," her mother chastised. "You've been back a week and this is the first we've heard from you. I was beginning to think you'd forgotten you had parents."

"Sorry, but I do have a job to do and it's been full on since I got back," Kim explained. "The first couple of days, I was just floating through the time zone so to speak. It took all my strength and concentration to function on the urgent work that had to be done. Next time I'll sort out my schedule properly."

"There's going to be a next time?" Belinda asked, trying not to show her anxiety.

"I think it will be a fairly regular trip from now on. My links with OTA are taking off big time and both Simon Obertelli and I will have to make visits here and there if we intend to succeed in our joint ventures. We are going to set up an exchange programme for new artistes. It's our baby…" She paused and smiled to herself at the implication of her analogy. "…and we want to watch it develop and grow into a world class organisation. It's very exciting."

Belinda didn't know what to think or say. "Oh," she offered.

"Is that all you can say, Mum? It's a fantastic idea. I would have thought you'd appreciate the scale of the operation. Simon says…"

"Simon? Simon? Is he somebody special over there?" Belinda asked warily and yet with a touch of irritation in her voice that she couldn't hide.

"He's the managing director of OTA. His father is Shane Obertelli and he's the person who has dealt with Theo Pendennis in the past. Didn't Dad tell you when I called from Perth?" Kim said. "Simon and I…"

"Is there something going on with you and this Simon person?" Belinda asked bluntly.

Kim went quiet. *Do I tell her, or do I keep her in the dark?* "We are very good friends," she cautiously revealed.

"Kim?" Belinda questioned pointedly.

"Mum?" Kim answered in exactly the same tone as her mother.

Belinda's irritation was growing by the second. "Don't you dare play that game with me, young lady," she scolded. "Tell me what is going on."

"Simon and I have fallen in love," Kim ventured tentatively. "It didn't happen straight away, but it developed during my stay."

"It's just a holiday romance, isn't it? Once you've been home for a while, it will all fizzle out," Belinda said and not without a touch of venom in her voice which was not lost on Kim.

"What's with you, Mother?" she snapped. "I'm not a child and I am quite capable of knowing my own feelings and leading my own life. We intend to make this relationship work, both professionally and personally. Do you have a problem with that?"

Belinda snapped back. "No, you are not a child, but it seems you have no common sense. How on earth can you continue a relationship with ten thousand miles between you? It's madness and you know it. You certainly won't get my blessing to continue a relationship with somebody in Australia." She took a deep breath and then spat out, "Australia of all places."

"I don't need your personal blessing, Mother. Just you remember that," she said caustically. "And from now on, don't expect me to keep you informed of my whereabouts, because it's not going to happen. This is *my* life, *my* way." She stopped abruptly and shivered. *Those words again and I'm trembling.* She breathed in deeply. "I'm going now," she said, but she heard the phone click at the other end without her mother saying goodbye.

~ * ~

"I'm home," Ben called when he arrived in from work. The house was silent. "That's odd," he said out loud. "Belinda?" Still there was no response. He went into the kitchen where he found his wife sitting at the breakfast bar, her head in her hands. "Bel? What's the matter?"

Belinda lifted a tear-stained face and looked at Ben with sheer desperation in her eyes. "She's fallen in love with an Australian," she said quietly.

Ben sighed audibly. "I assume you're talking about Kimberley," he said.

"A bloody Australian!" Belinda said more loudly.

"Well, what's so wrong with that, babe?" Ben asked.

"She can't go to live in Australia. The risks would be too great. It will be the end of our family. She'll…"

"Calm down for goodness sake, Bel," Ben coaxed.

"She must be mad," she snapped. "And I told her so. We've had a row like never before. She more or less told me that my opinion means nothing to her. She isn't going to tell me what she's doing, or where she's going ever again."

"That's just Kim, isn't it? You know she doesn't like being told what to do."

"That's an understatement if ever there was one," Belinda rejoined. "Think about it, Ben. It's the same situation Joel had with *his* mother. God forbid she should take the same road through life as he did."

"Look, Bel, you can't blame Joel every time Kim does something you don't like. You know as well as I do that he has had absolutely no influence on her life…"

"She has his genes and that's enough for me," Belinda interrupted.

"I can't deny that and you take every opportunity to rub in the fact that he's her father and I'm not. I've done everything in my power to raise Kim as my daughter. I love her and I respect the person she has become, but I don't need you reminding me constantly that I had nothing to do with her conception." Ben was becoming angry and Belinda started to cry again. "And don't use your tears to soften me up. I'm over it, Bel. I suggest you get over it too, or it will be the end of us and it will be your fault, not Kim's and not Joel's. Enough is enough!"

"But Australia, Ben! She's bound to run into Joel sometime if she's over there permanently."

"Don't be so bloody ridiculous, Bel. How many times does that situation have to be explained to you?" He stormed out of the house, slamming the door behind him.

~ * ~

Kimberley went to sit on her deck. It was dark and cold, but she didn't care. She pulled her coat around her and stared out at the Thames gently flowing past the bottom of her garden. The water looked black and deep—*Just like my thoughts,* she mused. She tried to understand the reasoning behind her mother's attitude. When she couldn't comprehend any of it, she felt an overwhelming need to call Simon.

"Hello?" he said sleepily.

"Hi, baby..."

"Kim? Is that you?" Simon asked, suddenly more awake.

"Did I waken you?" she asked. "I'm sorry, but I needed to talk to you." She couldn't hide the distress in her voice.

"What's the matter, baby? You sound sad."

"I told my mother about you tonight and she..." *How can I explain to Simon when I don't understand it myself?*

"I guess she doesn't approve then. Is it because I'm Italian? Are there religious issues? I don't understand how she can disapprove of me when she hasn't met me," he reasoned.

"No, it's not you, darl. I really don't know what it is. It's something to do with Australia. She was against me coming out to see you in the first place. She didn't say it in so many words, but she was suggesting alternatives like it's too far to go to see performers I know nothing about and she was adamant that I should just ask for demo discs. Why would she do that? What would *she* know about this business?" Kim was both talking fast and trying to make sense of her mother's attitude at the same time.

Simon sat up in his bed. "It's four-fifteen in the morning here, baby, so my brain isn't functioning properly," he told her.

"Oh my goodness! I didn't work out what time it would be for you, babe. I'm so sorry," she apologised. "I'm being selfish and should have been more considerate. I'm really sorry, baby."

"No need to apologise, sweetheart. I'm here for you whatever the time of day or night. Maybe your mum doesn't like the thought of you travelling all this way on your own. Didn't you say you had come over as a family years ago? She would obviously know what a gruelling trip it is." He was clutching at straws. "I know *my* mother would lie awake worrying about me in a similar situation. That's what mothers do, isn't it?"

Kim sighed. "I don't think it's that. I've travelled all over Europe and I went to New York a couple of times so she's used to me going off on my own. No, there's something more and I don't for the life of me know what it is."

"Maybe when you've slept on it, it won't seem half so bad," Simon offered.

"Perhaps you're right," she agreed. "I'm angry with her right now, but thanks for letting me unburden myself on you, darl."

"That's what I'm here for, baby, and don't forget, a problem shared is a…"

"…problem halved," she interrupted. "Thank you, Mr. Cliché King," she joked, grateful for the levity.

"Well, at least I'm hearing a more cheerful Kimberley now," he told her, "but, darl, I really must try to go back to sleep right now. I need to be up early in the morning, but I'll call you when I get to the office."

"Oh, sorry, babe," she said quietly. "You go back to sleep. I love you. Sleep tight and dream of me being in your arms."

"I will and I will," he told her and gently replaced the phone on the hook.

Thirteen

Ben walked around the park for what seemed like hours. His mind was blank for much of the time. Only when he felt relaxed again did he think of calling Kim to find out what was going on. He felt in his pocket for his mobile phone. "Hi, sweetheart," he said, but his voice did not convey his usual happy self.

Kim was still angry. "Dad, if you've called to tell me off, don't bother. I'm fed up of having to pussyfoot around Mum in order to keep her happy. For the past few months, it seems I can't do anything right and I'm sick of it."

Ben realised he would have to choose his words carefully. "I have no idea what is going on, Kim," he told her. "Well, that's not strictly true, but I don't know what has caused you and your mum to have this almighty row. She's pretty distraught about it and thinks you're never going to speak to her again."

"Has she got you to call me?" Kim asked, not trying to hide her irritation.

"No, she hasn't. She doesn't even know where I am. I've had to come out of the house to get some air," he admitted. "Sometimes I can't handle her moods and just recently she's been up and down like a yo-yo. Maybe she's menopausal."

"Could be, but I'm not so sure it's hormonal. It all started when I told her I was going to Australia. She has this massive hang-up about it and wants to put obstacles in my way all the time," Kim complained. "I don't understand it and when I told her about Simon…"

"Hold on, who's Simon?"

"Simon Obertelli. He's the MD of OTA and we have fallen in love."

"Oh, I see," Ben said. "I was right then about the son, wasn't I? How serious is it?"

"Serious enough," Kim told him without divulging her innermost feelings.

Ben didn't know how to play it. *We're treading on dangerous ground here,* he thought. "Perhaps your mum doesn't want you living at the other side of the world. Is that what caused the friction?"

"No, it's more than that. She didn't know about Simon when she started all this. *I* didn't know about Simon when she first showed her disapproval of all things Australian," she said, again trying to elicit some information from her father. "Can't you shed any light on it, Dad?"

"I'll talk to your mum," he said noncommittally.

Kim sighed. "Good luck with that then" she said. "It seems every time I mention Australia, I hit a blank wall. Why have we never talked about our family trip to the Antipodes years ago? I can't remember anything about it except being a bridesmaid for your friend. I had a kind of flashback a few months ago, and…"

Ben interrupted. "Let's not talk about that just now, Kim. It's your mum we need to worry about. I don't like you being at loggerheads with her all the time."

Kim tutted loudly. "There you go again," she complained. "Australia is mentioned and you try to divert my attention. What is wrong with you two?"

"Please, Kim, not now. We'll talk about it later, I promise, but just not now."

"I won't give up, Dad. There's something going on and I intend to get to the bottom of it," she told him adamantly.

"Okay, sweetheart. I'd better go home and see how your mum is coping now that she's had time to calm down. All I want you to remember is that I love you; we both do."

"I know that, Dad. You are the best; always have been, always will be," she said, her voice filled with emotion.

~ * ~

In Perth, Western Australia, Joel Winston was working his three months' notice with the television company that had made his name in Australia. "I'm going to miss the thrill of performing and filming," he told Marti Brannigan, his present production assistant, "But it's time for me to move on."

"We'll miss you too, but I guess you'll find us the talent we need, when we need it. The *Performing for Australia* show coming out of Sydney seems to be a big hit and the Obertelli Agency is involved in a big way."

"I know," Joel said. "It reminds me of *Have You Got What It Takes?* all those years ago. I shall be eternally grateful for that show and to Shane Obertelli for bringing me out here. I met him when I was working on the cruise ships."

~ * ~

"How do you do, sir?" Joel greeted him.

"I'm good, young man and very pleased to meet you. Congratulations on your performances. I have been very impressed," the passenger informed him. He was Australian and on his way home to Melbourne on the cruise ship after a trip to

London in search of new talent. "To be honest, I was beginning to think I had made a wasted trip until I saw you. All the young Poms are into rock 'n' roll these days and I need an all-round performer —like you, Joel Winston —good name, by the way."

Joel laughed at that, but he was confused and it showed. "Thank you very much, but ..."

"Jeez! I'm a real goose," the man said, "Sorry. I'm Shane Obertelli. I work for the TV Network operating out of Melbourne, but we're setting up a station in Perth.

~ * ~

Joel completed his three months' notice and decided to give himself four weeks off before contacting the Obertelli Agency to make arrangements for the Perth branch to open. "We'll spend some quality time together," he informed his wife, "before I start travelling around WA in search of new talent."

Sheralyn sighed. "I don't know how I feel, darl," she told him. "We have never spent time apart in the past twenty years other than when we've been at work during the day, but soon you'll be going off without me and I'm not sure I'm going to like it."

Joel took her hand across the breakfast table. "I wish I could say come with me, but it wouldn't be feasible. With Glenn at uni and Helena and Jasmine still in school, you have to be home with them. I'll try to keep the travelling down to a minimum and in lots of cases it will just be local auditions, visits to theatre schools and to dance academies to spot emerging talent in its embryonic stage. I'm really excited about that."

Sheralyn regarded her husband through affectionate eyes. "I've not seen you so enthusiastic for a long time," she said, "and that makes me happy, babe. Just go for it! Now I have to do the school run on my way to work. Some of us still have a job to do." She smiled lovingly at her husband and blew him a kiss as she left the room. "Come on, girls," she called. "We're going to be late."

~ * ~

Ben returned to the house not knowing what to expect of his wife. "Bel," he called out gently.

She didn't respond and Ben sighed deeply. He looked in the kitchen where he had left her just half an hour ago, but she wasn't there. "Bel?" he called again, louder this time. He opened the lounge door to find her curled up on the hearth rug, hugging her knees as though she were physically holding herself together. He approached her cautiously. "Bel?" he whispered as he took her arm and pulled her towards him. Enfolding her in his arms, he gently rocked her to try to comfort her. "Come on, baby," he coaxed. "This is not the Belinda I know, the strong, competent Belinda who copes with whatever life throws at her."

"I can't do it anymore, Ben. I'm tired of hiding the past. Not telling Kim the truth is going to destroy me, destroy us," she told him wearily.

"Are you saying what I think you are saying?" he asked tentatively.

Belinda looked at him with desperation in her eyes. "I think I am," she conceded. "I can't cope with it anymore. I'm losing Kim now because I haven't told her the truth, and if I do tell her the truth, I'll lose her anyway. I'm in a no-win situation."

"You can't be sure of that," Ben said. "How do we know how she'll react?"

Belinda sat up straight, an action that demonstrated she was regaining her confidence. "Come on, Ben," she said bluntly. "We know exactly how she'll react. Kim will explode and accuse us of lying, of cowardice; of mental abuse."

"What?" Ben exclaimed. "How can you say that word in the same breath as Kimberley's name Band our attachment to her? I find that despicable, Bel. We've never abused her in any way, shape, or form."

"Obviously we know that, but will she?" Belinda asked plaintively. "She'll misconstrue our actions, our motives and our love. That's the way she is, Ben. She's her father's daughter, hot-headed and strong-willed and we can't get away from that however much we would like to."

Ben was thoughtful. Eventually he said, "We have to think this through, Bel. I called her while I was out..."

"Oh, brilliant," Belinda said sarcastically.

"If we're being honest, we have to start now, this minute and not shy away from the truth anymore," he stated forcefully. "She has already made the connection that Australia is causing the problem. I warded her away from it, but she detected that too. I promised I would talk to you and discuss Australia later."

"Oh great," Belinda said, her tone still laced with sarcasm.

Ben sighed audibly. "If we're going to tell the truth, it has to be the whole truth. It's bound to be traumatic for us, but for Kim, it will shatter her whole world. We have to be sure we're doing what is right, not for us this time, but for Kim.

Now it was Belinda's turn to sigh. "I hear you, Ben, but..."

"No buts, Bel. We can't be selfish anymore. This is our daughter we're talking about and I think she deserves to know the truth."

Fourteen

By the end of April, Kim had secured bookings for the Australian acts in the UK and in Europe. "I'm completely up to schedule with everything," she informed Simon the day she signed all the contracts with the relevant parties. "I'll book my flight for the end of the week."

"That's great, baby. Shall I tell James Radicchio you'll actually be available for the end of May?" he asked, the excitement evident in every word.

"I guess so," she said resignedly. "but I'm still not completely sure I'm cut out for television, but I do know my job and it will be wonderful exposure for Premier Plus and for our exchange programme when it takes off."

"That's very true, darl, but all that's filling my head at the moment is that we'll be together again. Shall I book a room at the Hilton? Don't forget, it's all expenses paid," Simon reminded her. "You could stay at the Obertelli house, but I want you all to myself. They all know about us now so there won't be any objection to my being away from home for a while."

Kim sighed deeply. "I wish I could say the same about my family," she declared. "I haven't spoken to my parents for weeks. I'm not ready yet to offer the olive branch to Mum. She is the one who is out of order here. Tony called to say the house was like a morgue, cold and uninspiring. He is spending most of his time at Liz's house. They won't discuss anything with him either. Mum is miserable all the time and Dad tries to put on a brave face. Apparently, he asked Tony to call to tell me to lie low for a while."

"Sounds awful, baby. Is there anything I can do?"

"Thanks, sweetheart, but no. We'll get all this sorted sometime. Dad will be in control as usual," she said. "He has always been there for me and I know he'll have my best interests at heart as well as Mum's. I trust him implicitly."

"Perhaps coming here will be good for you all. It will give you some space and time to reflect on the situation. I can't wait to see you."

"I think I'll do an overnight stop in Singapore this time. It will break the journey and help me recover from the jet lag more quickly. The travel agent booked me in at the Singapore Sheraton Hotel. I thought I'd splash out and have the luxury."

"Okay, babe. Sounds wonderful. Won't be long now," he said, but he couldn't prevent his heart from beating wildly in his chest and his brain planning his next move.

~ * ~

In their Bolton home, Ben and Belinda Mason struggled to keep some semblance of normality in their day to day routine. Work was a welcome break for both of them, but evenings were fraught with unfinished business and unspoken tensions.

Their son, Tony, had discreetly kept Ben informed of what was happening in Kim's life. Ben, himself, drew upon all his resources to work out the correct way to deal with the Kimberley situation.

"We have to decide what we are going to do, Bel," he said as soon as he felt his wife was ready to deal with it.

"I know I have to face whatever comes," she said pointedly. "For thirty years I have kept a close guard on what happened in Liverpool that fateful afternoon. When you rescued me from the brink of despair, I appreciated so much what you were doing for me. How can I ever repay you for that?"

"I loved you, Bel. What else could I do? And you have repaid me a thousand fold in being my wife and the mother of my children."

"I know you love me and I feel so ashamed that I didn't love you at that time, but I love you now, Ben, truly I do. I need you to believe that. We convinced everybody you were the father of my baby, even my parents. They'd be turning in their graves now if they knew the truth," Belinda disclosed openly for the first time. "I know too how much the loyalty of Penny and Gerry means. They have kept my secret for my sake all these years. They could quite easily have let it slip, but they didn't. How many friends would be so loyal?"

Ben took her hand and squeezed it gently to reassure her. "We have to believe we did what we thought was right at the time," he explained. "But now it's different. Circumstances have changed. Hints that something is wrong have surfaced."

"That's my fault, I know," Belinda conceded.

"I'm not laying any blame at your door, Bel," he reassured her. "We, as human beings, are all vulnerable to the vagaries of life. *My* ultimate aim in life was to cast away the stigma of having parents like mine, a father who left two children behind through his own selfishness and a mother who had no morals and no sense whatsoever of family values. I know I have done what I set out to do, but as regards Kim, how were we to anticipate her job would take her to Australia? It's pure coincidence and we have no control over that."

Belinda looked at him directly. "I have to say this, Ben, and believe me, I'm not getting at you in any way, but Kim has more of Joel in her than we have dared to acknowledge."

"I know that. I've seen it and ignored it," he admitted. "We have even encouraged some of the Winston traits."

"How do you mean encouraged?"

"We both urged her to take piano lessons; we took her to the theatre; we sent her to dance classes and we encouraged her to take that part-time job at the Royal Theatre. All those things were unwittingly inspired by Joel Winston. We knew about his theatrical background and we still went ahead with encouraging Kim to get involved in the theatre. If you hadn't told her about the advertisement in the paper, perhaps none of this would have materialised." Ben was trying to make sense of the situation.

Belinda looked sad. "What's done is done," she said. "Now we have to make things right, although I feel sick at the thought of relating my lurid past to my daughter, but I do agree with you; she has the right to know the truth. We'll just have to live with the consequences, but it breaks my heart to think she might cut us out of her life forever."

"I know, darling," Ben said. They were not just as words of agreement, but more as words of comfort, "We made our bed... " He paused. "I'll contact her as soon as she returns from her trip."

Fifteen

After thirteen hours on a Qantas flight, Kim touched down in Singapore at eight o'clock the following morning. The air outside was warm and humid, but Changi Airport was fresh, clean and inviting. *I'm so pleased I decided on a stop-over,* she thought. *I'll spend the day chilling out; I'll call Simon and then I'll go to Raffles for dinner.* She felt the cool air from the air con on her face as she went down the steps to baggage collection. *Ah, good, plenty of taxis at the front. Strange being able to see them from here. I hope the taxi drivers can speak English.*

She collected her cases and placed them on a trolley. "Carry your bags, Miss?" the voice said behind her. She stopped in her tracks.

"Simon!" she exclaimed. "What on earth are you doing here?"

Explanations were unnecessary. Simon took her in his arms and held her close, nuzzling her hair and whispering in her ear. "You smell so good," he said tenderly. "I just had to meet you here. I couldn't wait until you arrived in Sydney. After you told me where you were staying, I contacted the hotel and made sure it was a double room."

"You sneaky person; sneaky, conniving, deceitful, wonderful person," she said as she smothered him with kisses. "Though I don't know how romantic I can be after that marathon flight," she teased.

"I can wait. Just go to sleep in my arms and then I'll take you to Raffles for dinner tonight."

"Are you psychic or something? I was planning to go to Raffles myself, but now that you're here, it will be all the more special. We can't be in Singapore and not visit that monumental establishment."

"No, we cannot, but what do you think of my first real venture out of Australia? My brother can no longer jest about my lack of travel experience. I'm halfway to England already!"

"Indeed you are, baby," Kim said with affection. "Now let's get to the hotel before I fall asleep on my feet."

Five hours later, after a short nap and some passionate love-making, they showered and dressed before taking a leisurely stroll from the hotel through the hustle and bustle of the Singapore streets. They found it both relaxing and entertaining just to wander around exquisite shops and experience the different cultures that Singapore had to offer. Back at the hotel, they made love again before the anticipated visit to the Raffles Tiffin Room for typical Indian and Asian cuisine.

"This is the best curry I have ever tasted," Kim remarked. "It is so delicious."

Main course over, Simon suggested dessert. "You have to have dessert, Kim. I've heard they are out of this world."

"I don't think I could fit in another mouthful," she cried. "I'm absolutely stuffed!"

"But you have to, otherwise the meal will not be complete," he told her, almost pleading.

Just as she was about to argue her point, the white-coated waiter arrived with a special gateau and a little parcel on his tray. "Oh, my goodness," she exclaimed, "This is surely the icing on the cake. It looks like Raffles gives favours just like we get at weddings. What a lovely gesture!"

When the waiter discreetly disappeared, Simon stood up and went round to her side of the table. "Let me help you open your surprise," he said as he took the package and untied the silk ribbon that adorned it.

Kim was bemused. "What's going on?" she asked, a curious smile on her flushed face.

Simon took hold of the little box inside the package and opened it. He knelt beside Kim.

"Kimberley Mason," he said, "will you marry me?"

"Are you serious?" she asked.

"I have never been so serious in my life. I love you, Kim, and I would like us to spend the rest of our lives together. Please say you'll be my wife."

Kim was lost for words. She was smiling and looking first at Simon then at the ring, back and forth until she collected her thoughts.

"Kim, please answer me. The suspense is killing me."

She shook her head slowly, still with a beaming smile on her face. Simon's expression changed from eager anticipation to anxious doubt.

"This is madness, Simon, but somehow I know it will work," she said, surprise and excitement evident in her voice. "So..." She paused. "My answer is...YES!"

Simon removed the diamond solitaire ring from the box and placed it on her finger to the applause of the Raffles' staff, who had stood at a discreet distance to watch the proceedings. "I know we have a lot of planning to do, baby," Simon acknowledged, "but we'll make it work. I just know it. First of all, we have to prepare you for your television debut in a couple of weeks' time. It's going to be great."

Kim looked at the man she loved with all her heart. "I just hope I can deliver the goods now that you have talked me up to James Radicchio," she told him.

"I know you will, baby. I just know you will."

~ * ~

"*Performing for Australia* is on again tonight. We must watch it so I can see what I'm going to be looking for," Joel told Sheralyn as she left for work. "I'll make dinner and we can open a bottle of wine to celebrate my newfound freedom."

"I wouldn't call it freedom, darl," Sheralyn replied. "It's just a holiday before your work starts all over again. Enjoy it while you may. But dinner made for me will be wonderful." She smiled lovingly at her husband. "See you later. Bye."

Joel spent all day in his studio. *Just because I'm not going out to work doesn't mean I shouldn't work on my music,* he thought. *I think I'll sort out my demo discs first and then see what little gem I can come up with to celebrate my temporary retirement.* He started at the top of the rack and found the very first disc he'd cut--*Flight of Fancy*. "Wow," he said out loud. "This was written for part of my music exam at school and I used it as one of my audition pieces at Maria Morenzi's in Liverpool. I remember the first time I sang it for the Connollys."

They sat in the cosy living room for a couple of hours listening to this young lad who had appeared from nowhere and was allowing them to be privy to his talent before his audition. Joel's confidence soared with their appreciation and he decided his audition pieces would be Can't Help Falling in Love, the Elvis' version, Cliff Richard's Nine Times Out of Ten, which would give more scope to show his pop side and then he would finish with his own composition, Flight of Fancy. The words would be perfect:

'There's a place in my heart where fantasy dwells,
There is hope that I'll always be free,
To follow my vision that gives me the chance,
To follow that dear flight of fancy.

Chorus: Don't say it's a pipedream,
Don't tell me I'm wrong,
Don't shatter illusions
When I sing you my song.

There's a wish that I'm wishing deep in my soul,
There's a consuming yearning within,
Belief ever urging and making me dance
To the tune of my dear flight of fancy.

Chorus: Don't say etc.'

His memories were so clear. "They were the good times, before the demons appeared," he said and he shivered. "Time to clear my head now and write something new."

When Sheralyn arrived home, dinner was ready and the television already on to await the start of *Performing for Australia*. "I thought we would slum it tonight and eat from trays on our laps."

"How refined," Sheralyn joked. "What about the kids?"

"All out tonight. Glenn is crashing at William's; Helena is staying with Anna, and Jasmine has gone to Holly's pyjama party. That means we have the house to ourselves and we can completely monopolise the remote control," he stated with a grin. "We'd better make the most of it, because that doesn't happen very often."

"We ought to consider getting them bigger televisions for their bedrooms. The portables are obsolete now, according to them.

And these new flat screens are what every kid wants these days. That's why we never get a chance to watch the big TV in peace!" she explained light-heartedly.

"I'm not buying them yet. They're too expensive for them to have one each and apart from that, too much TV is bad for them."

"That's rich coming from a person who has made his living in television," Sheralyn quipped.

"I know, but my stuff was good, wholesome family TV, not the inane, crass stuff some stations put out these days."

Sheralyn looked at her husband and smiled knowingly. "I guess three brand new television sets would be a bit extravagant," she agreed. "Anyway, Glenn is already talking about going over to the Gold Coast when he's qualified."

"To live with Mum and Sean?" Joel interrupted. "Well, that's a turn up. I point blank refused to live with my grandparents in Liverpool when I left home."

"It seems you refused to do a lot of things when you were a teenager," Sheralyn reminded him.

"Yes, well, it was all a very big learning curve for me."

"I'm in Liverpool, not a million miles away and it's a place I'm familiar with so you've no need to worry. Please don't make this any more difficult for me, Mum." Joel was still not in the mood for his mother's antics, but felt he should at least try to be civil.

"But where will you stay? Couldn't you live at Granny and Grandpa's? It's only a ferry ride to the city centre. I think that would be ideal and..."

"You still don't get it, do you, Mum? You think it would be ideal, your decision, your choice. All this has to be my choice and my decision. If I make mistakes, they'll be my mistakes and I'll deal with them," Joel insisted. "I'm going to apply for a place at the City Theatre School, so I'll let you know how it goes. Bye for now, Mum." He replaced the receiver before Nell played the emotional card again. He wasn't ready for all that sob-story stuff just yet.

"Yoohoo!" Sheralyn broke into his thoughts. "The programme is starting."

Joel made himself comfortable as the fanfare began to open the show. The presenter, a young man by the name of Ryan Fortune, had appeared on Joel's show *Have You Got What It Takes?* many years ago. Now he was an established presenter and Joel felt a proud affiliation to him. "This kid's good," he commented to Sheralyn and then he suddenly fell silent.

Ryan continued to introduce the judges. "And tonight for the first time on Australian television, we welcome from London, England, the much respected owner of the renowned Premier Plus Theatrical Agency..."

Joel's heart missed a beat and then it began to pound in his chest as Ryan enthusiastically continued with his introduction.

"M-i-s-s Kimberley M-a-s-o-n!"

Sixteen

They watched the show in complete silence, each with their own thoughts. When it had finished, Joel went to sit on the deck and Sheralyn knew she had to leave him alone. She, herself, was weighed down with confused images in her head. *The girl looks just like Joel; she's the spitting image of him. What do we do now? What if the children saw the show? What do we tell them? Surely they will see the likeness. It's incredible. Even our little Jasmine, who, out of all of our three children, most resembles her father, doesn't look anything like Kimberley Mason. Oh my God.*

Joel sat in silence for a while when the show had finished. *That was the girl I saw at the airport,* he reflected. *No wonder I felt that somebody had walked over my grave. Bloody hell...* He breathed in deeply. *She's good at her job, though,* and he smiled to himself as he breathed deeply again. Suddenly the reality of the situation set in.

Sheralyn dared to sit with him and spoke first. "What do we do now, babe?" she asked gently.

Joel took her hand more for reassurance than out of affection, although he loved her dearly. "I don't know. I guess we do nothing, but the implications are massive. She must have connections with the Obertelli Agency. They have strong links with the show. If she's met Shane Obertelli, he will surely have seen the likeness. It's creepy, isn't it? It's like looking at the female version of me. Bloody hell, Sher, I don't know what I should do."

~ * ~

After a restless night, the Winstons sat bleary eyed at the breakfast table, trying to decipher what had happened the night before. Then the telephone rang. "I'll give you one guess who that will be," Sheralyn told him. "She'll just have watched the recording. She said they had a function to attend and wouldn't be watching the show live. Do you want me to put her off?"

Joel sighed. "No. I'll get it," he said resignedly. "My mother will not let it rest until she's said her piece. She's always like a dog with a bone, so I may as well face the music and get it over with."

"Did you see the show?" Nell shrieked at the other end of the line. "My God, Joel, it's unbelievable! Did you know anything about her links with theatrical agencies? Does she know about you? Have you been in touch with her over the years and never told me? If you have, Joel Winston, I'll never forgive..."

"Slow down, Mum, or you'll give yourself a heart attack," he said in an effort to diffuse the situation. "Yes, I saw the show; no, I didn't know about her job and no, I have not been in touch with her, or Ben, or Belinda. As far as I know, she thinks Ben is her father and that's how it has to remain."

"But..."

"No buts, Mother. It's the way it is and the way it stays. Don't you even think about making contact," he told the obviously excited Nell. "Promise me you won't do anything irresponsible."

"That's just what Sean said to me. I have had this very strong feeling that Kimberley is what is missing from my life and it all evolved from the involuntary flashbacks I told you about when you were here. It's a bit spooky really, but I have to say, Joel, we can't just ignore the fact that she is here in Australia and is heavily involved in the same business as you are. How coincidental is that?"

Joel sighed. "Mother," he said pointedly, "That's all it is—coincidence. I'm as shocked as you are, but we must keep our promise to Ben and Belinda. At first I didn't know what to do, but it's obvious now that I've had time to think about it. A promise is a promise, especially one with all the ramifications this one presents. There is absolutely no way I would ever contact Kimberley Mason. Coming face-to-face with her would be a disaster."

~ * ~

"Good show, baby," Simon greeted her after the first of her television appearances. "You handled it like an old pro!"

Kim laughed. "I called my mum an old pro once and Dad almost had convulsions."

"Why would your mum have been an old pro?" he asked.

"Apparently she had somehow dabbled in the world of entertainment at one time. Dad mentioned it when I was applying for the job with Premier Plus. She never discussed it with me and she never mentioned that she had been interested in becoming an entertainer. That's another odd thing about her. I'm beginning to think she has something to hide. I have no idea what it is, but I intend to find out eventually."

Simon gave her a hug. "Let's not think about that now, sweetheart. We have your television debut to celebrate."

The next few days were idyllic. With a week between programmes going to air, Kim and Simon had time to spend getting to know each other better and they used the time for Kim to explore Sydney and begin to feel a part of the vibrant city life. "I love it," she announced as they returned from a coffee cruise around the harbour. "It's so easy to feel a part of everything. I love the place, the people and the lifestyle."

"That's good, babe, because eventually, we'll have to share our time between Sydney and London. If we are going to make it work both professionally and personally, we'll have to know exactly where we are heading."

"I know that, darling, but for the time being, let's just familiarise ourselves with each other."

"I'm all for that," Simon replied with a twinkle in his eye.

"Well, what are we waiting for?" she asked. "Let's go!"

~ * ~

Joel Winston's phone rang a couple of days after the last showing of *Performing for Australia*. "Hello, Joel Winston here."

The voice at the other end of the line boomed out. "Joel, you old bastard, how are you?"

"How are you, Shane? And not so much of the old," he said light-heartedly. "I'll put up with the bastard bit, because I've become Australianised now after all this time, but you know us Poms; we take offence at the slightest thing and I refuse to accept that I could ever be regarded as OLD!" Joel told Obertelli. "What can I do for you?"

"Did you see the show?" Shane asked.

"I did."

"What did you think?"

Joel took his time to answer. *Think on your feet, Joel,* he said silently to himself. *There are implications that Shane Obertelli can't possibly have any idea about.* "I thought it was top notch, a vast improvement on my original show, but that's exactly what I would expect. I've liked the idea all along that there are on-the-spot critiques from the judges," he said cautiously.

"I like that aspect too. The Australian guys, Alex Levine and Eddie Davidson, were good, but I think the young girl from the UK was outstanding."

Joel had to think quickly again. "She was very good," he said almost non-committal.

"Bloody hell, Joel," Shane responded, "She was better than very good. Surely you could recognise her unbiased appraisal and complete understanding of the business. It will be a coup for OTA when she signs the contract for her company to amalgamate with us. Not only that, she's seeing my son, Simon, so it looks like we'll certainly be keeping it in the family."

Joel was stunned. "Congratulations," he said without emotion.

Shane was openly candid. "She's Theo Pendennis's protégée. She'll be an asset, that's for sure. And what a looker she is! She's got your colouring, Joel. You'd better warn your lovely wife before the public start making assumptions," he joked. "If I didn't know better, *I* might have assumed you had something to do with her existence too. The resemblance is uncanny."

"Ha, ha," Joel managed to reply. "Very funny, Shane, very bloody funny." His heart was thumping in his chest. *Theo Pendennis? How many more shocks do I have to take?*

~ * ~

He had been sitting there for about ten minutes before the door behind the desk opened again. A very tall, theatrical looking gentleman appeared wearing a crisp white shirt and sporting a very colourful cravat around his neck. His very upright stance gave him an air of superiority and Joel assumed he was the principal. "Good morning, young man," he said offering a well-manicured hand. "Theodore Pendennis."

Smiling confidently, he replied, "Good morning, Sir. I'm pleased to meet you."

"Let me see your application, please. You must be keen if you've come here to apply in person. I like a bit of initiative."

Theodore Pendennis studied the sheet in silence apart from the intermittent grunts that didn't inspire Joel with confidence at all. "Hmm, O level results pretty impressive. That's useful because you have to do theory in some of our subjects, particularly music." He paused briefly and took out a large desk diary from under the counter. Flicking through the pages, he said, "Let's see, are you able to come back on Friday for an audition?"

"Yes, Sir," Joel replied enthusiastically.

"Bring references and make sure you have audition pieces prepared. Four-thirty Friday, and your name?"

"Joel Winston, Sir."

"Hmm, that's a posh name. A good stage name. See you on Friday and please be punctual." With a flourish of his right hand, Theodore Pendennis exited stage left.

Back in the present, Joel shivered involuntarily. *There is something very weird about this,* he thought, *something very, very weird.*

~ * ~

Nell Flynn was restless. *I can't just sit here and do nothing,* she thought. *Surely as a grandmother I have some rights. It's all very well Sean and Joel telling me not to do anything reckless. What's so reckless about wanting to meet my grand-daughter?* She shifted on her sun-lounger and drew up her knees. Wrapping her arms around her legs and resting her chin on her knees, she stared out across the river, focussing on nothing in particular. Her mind was in turmoil. *In the old days, I would have had a drink to help clear my head. These days, one glass of wine would probably kill me. I daren't go down that road again, but God, do I need a drink just now!*

Sean found her in pensive mood. "You're looking as though you have the worries of the world on your shoulders. Anything I can do to help?"

"Not really. I still can't get over how Kimberley appeared on TV almost as soon as I'd been thinking about her. It's quite eerie."

"What's eerie about it?" Sean asked.

"If I were into all that psychic stuff, I'd say I had the gift. This is not a joke, but a serious assessment. I tell you, Sean, it's eerie."

"Coincidence, Nell, pure coincidence just as Joel said. I know it must be frustrating for you, but we really do have to respect Ben and Belinda's wishes. Who's to say what a can of worms you would open if you contacted their daughter. There are too many people's lives involved here. Ben and Belinda had another child whom we have to suppose knows nothing of Kimberley's biological father neither. Imagine what it would do to Kimberley herself if you disclosed information that has never been given to her by her parents. It really doesn't bear thinking about." Sean looked at his wife, whose eyes were full of unshed tears.

Nell shook her head slowly. "In the meantime, we have to live with the fact that she'll never know who we are. It's pretty hard to take, Sean."

"I know, baby, but that's exactly what we have to do," Sean averred. "It isn't up to us, or more to the point, it isn't up to *you* to disclose the facts of Kimberley's parentage. Joel gave up the right of being her father almost thirty years ago. Ben is named as the father on the birth certificate, so short of DNA testing, Joel would have absolutely no proof of his involvement, even if he wanted to include himself in her life at this point. I firmly believe he has no intention of interfering in the lives of the Masons, so we have to respect Joel's wishes as well as theirs."

Nell's half smile displayed a touch of regret. "You know, the old Nell wouldn't have given a damn what other people might think. She would have dived head first into the situation regardless of whom she was hurting on the way. I hear you, Sean, but there is some of the old Nell urging me to contact that missing part of my family. After all, hasn't she voluntarily appeared in our lives, an appearance that was unexpected and uninvited? Fate has played a very big part in that."

Sean was aghast. "For Pete's sake, Nell, please don't do anything that will alienate you from Joel again. I beg you, don't do it."

Nell sighed. "Common sense tells me not to contact her, but my heart is beating so fast at the thought of welcoming Kimberley Mason into our family. I promise I will do as you ask, but something tells me that we'll meet eventually. I just know it."

Seventeen

Simon decided to return to the UK with Kim when her television appearances were over for the time being. "Dad has agreed to take over the Sydney office for a couple of months so I'll be able to learn the ropes Kimberley-style at Premier Plus," he told her. "Well, you did give me an invitation to stay with you when you came to the Obertelli house for dinner."

Kim grinned affectionately. "Maybe I'm psychic," she joked. "How could I possibly have known at that point that you were going to be my husband?" and she reached out across the breakfast table at the Hilton to squeeze his hand. "Tonight you must go home to organise your luggage and we'll spend a little time with your mum before we leave. Will she cope, do you think? I mean, her little boy is flying the nest at last!"

"She'll cope. All that little boy stuff is for show!" he said laughing. "She secretly can't wait to see the back of me!"

Mama O did indeed admit that she would be pleased to see Simon settled. "I have waited so long for this to happen, Kimberley," she said quietly as she and Kim sat in the kitchen while the men put the world to rights in the lounge room. "My Simon is a good boy. He'll make you a wonderful husband and together you will make beautiful bambinos." She stood and walked over to hug Kim affectionately. "Please love each other with all your hearts," she whispered. "That's all I ask."

Kim was touched. "We will and thank you, Mama O," she said, "I am so grateful you have accepted me." *A much more pleasant reaction than I got from my mother,* she thought sadly. *No wonder I haven't told her about our engagement yet. Well, her fault, not mine.* She smiled at Mama O. "I'll look after Simon," she assured her. "I promise."

~ * ~

The trip to London was much more bearable for Kim having Simon by her side. They tried to sleep, but as usual, the droning of the jet engines and the intermittent coughing and talking from the other passengers made it almost impossible to relax completely. She turned her head towards him and asked quietly, "Are you awake?"

"Yes. There's absolutely no way I can sleep. Not only do we have to put up with all the necessary plane noises, but I'm also too excited to sleep. This is my first trip to London, don't forget...and it's with you."

She rested her head on his shoulder and linked her arm through his. "You'll love it. We'll have such fun together...after work, of course!"

They landed at Heathrow, this time for Kim in beautiful July sunshine. Melissa was there to greet them. "Welcome home, Kim and welcome to sunny London, Simon. I am so pleased to meet you."

"I'm pleased to meet you too," he replied shaking her hand. "I'm looking forward to working with you."

Kim hugged Mel and then, taking Simon's hand, she led him through the sun-drenched car park to where her BMW was waiting. "I asked Mel to drive my car to the airport. I'd left it in the office car park while I was away. I'll let her drive us back there so you can see where we work. I don't know about you, but the jetlag hasn't hit me yet. I think I'm running on adrenalin."

"A big difference from last time," Melissa reminded her.

"I know," Kim agreed and then she spoke to Simon. "Last time I was cold and miserable, not to mention tired and stressed. I just burst into tears when I told Mel about you."

"Oh, how sweet!"

"I know. Mel had never seen me in such a state. Come to think of it, I had never been in such a state," she reasoned.

"All's well that ends well," he said and paused coyly. "Sorry, Kim."

Kim smiled at him affectionately. "I'll blame your Italian roots," she said and then explained to Melissa, "Clichés."

"She says it shows a lack of vocabulary." He smiled at Kim who pursed her lips and shook her head slowly.

"We all do it," Mel told him, "so don't worry about it."

On the journey to the office, Mel put them up to date with the two Australian acts. "Carousel has been jetting to and from Greece for the past six weeks. They are going great guns in Corfu and are appearing at the Agios Gordios Hotel on Saturday nights with a show at a night club in Ipsos on Sundays."

"That sounds awesome," Simon enthused.

"Not only that. They also have a regular spot every Wednesday at the NAAFI Club in Portsmouth. It's a lot of travelling, but they're young and seem to be having a whale of a time."

Kim appreciatively tapped Mel on the arm. "Well done, you," she said.

"Well done, you," Mel rejoined. "I'm just carrying out your instructions."

"What about Focus?" Simon asked.

"Oh, well that's another story," Mel told him. "They went to audition for the summer season at the Blackpool Opera House and were accepted straight away. They do seven shows a week, one every night except Sunday and a matinee on Saturday."

"Excellent," Kim and Simon said simultaneously.

"It doesn't end there, though," Mel continued. "An ITV rep saw them and has booked them for a new version of *Sunday Night at the London Palladium,* which also includes a whole season at the Palladium afterwards. That is absolutely brilliant...and all down to your hard work, Kimberley Mason."

"Did ITV actually contact us at Premier Plus?" Kim asked.

"They did everything right and so did Focus. There was no discussion between Focus and the ITV rep until she had contacted us. Gary Halsall represented you in your absence and he did a brilliant job."

"I guess that means he'll want a wage increase, but thanks, Mel. That's good news indeed."

By three o'clock in the afternoon, both Kim and Simon were the worse for wear. The jet lag kicked in with a vengeance and they decided they would leave the office and head home. "We'll go to the flat," she told Simon. "It's nearer and I'll leave the car here. Mel, will you call us a cab?"

The flat in Chelsea was luxurious and Simon was impressed. "This is quite something, Miss Mason," he said, "like something out of a movie."

"I'm very proud of it. As soon as I made enough money for the deposit, I jumped at the chance to buy. Six years on and it's mortgage free. My business took off and this place was a good investment."

They left their luggage in the entrance hall and literally fell into bed. Three hours later, they were wakened by the telephone ringing. "Hello?" Kim said sleepily.

"Kim. This is Dad…"

"Hi," she offered.

"How are you, princess?" Ben asked with as much love and affection as he could muster.

"I'm fine, Dad, but very jet lagged at the moment. Can I call you back later?"

"Okay, baby. We'll look forward to that. It's been so long."

"I know. I'll call when I'm more awake, Dad. Love you."

"I love you too, baby, more than you will ever know," and with that the phone went quiet.

~ * ~

Kim and Simon slept for hours. By eleven o'clock that evening, they were wide awake and ready to face the day. "This is hopeless," Kim declared. "When it's time to go to work, we'll be ready for bed again."

"I can't say I've experienced anything quite like this before," Simon said, "but I guess we eat, and then we do whatever takes our fancy."

"Simon!" she chastised.

Simon gave her a look of complete innocence. "Just a suggestion," he explained. "I thought it might use up our energies and then we could sleep again until morning time."

"Sounds like a good idea, but I have to think about talking to Dad," she told him. 'Seeing that he felt the need to phone as soon as we arrived home, I have to respond as soon as it's convenient. It's too late now. They'll be in bed. I'll call tomorrow before he goes out to work."

"If that's what you think is the right thing to do, Kim. You know best."

Simon's plan worked a treat. They ate smoked salmon and green salad, opened a bottle of red wine, made mad passionate love and went back to sleep until seven o'clock the following morning.

She called Bolton as soon as she got out of bed. "Hi Dad, it's me. I thought I'd catch you before you went to work," she said cheerily. "I'm feeling a bit brighter than I did last night."

"That's good," Ben replied. "Welcome home. How was the trip?"

"The trip was excellent. I did four TV appearances..."

"You did what?" Ben exclaimed. "You do surprise me. I would never have thought you'd have been in involved TV appearances. Well done, you. How did it go?"

"Brilliant as far as I can gather. Critiques were good. The Australians are very appreciative."

Ben was thinking on his feet again. *If Belinda knew this, she would go spare. Australia-wide TV coverage would not bode well for maintaining Kim's anonymity.* "We'd like to come down to see you," he told his daughter. "Is that okay?"

Kim was taken aback. "Wow, what brought this on?" she asked. "I can't remember the last time you visited me in London. I think it was when I bought Willow Bank and that was at least five years ago. If I remember correctly, Mum didn't like the hustle and bustle of London and when Mum doesn't like something..."

"Now, now, Kimberley," Ben warned. "No more of that."

"Sorry, but I'm not sure how to play it. Mum and I didn't part on very good terms," she conceded.

Ben chose his words carefully. "We would like to come to see you. There are things we need to explain."

"I agree with that," Kim stated. "I hope you can clarify a few things for me. When would you like to come down here?"

"We go *up* to the capital, Kim," her dad told her amicably, "even when we have to travel down south."

"I know that, but to common people like me, it sounds daft," she joked.

"Common? Never!" Ben rejoined. "When will it be convenient for you? Shall we book in a hotel? We don't want to invade your space."

"I have the room, Dad, so no, don't go to the expense of a hotel. The only thing is…" She paused. "Well, Simon is here and we have some news for you." She breathed in deeply. "We're engaged!"

Ben gasped audibly. "Well, I don't know what to say," he admitted. "Congratulations, I suppose. You really shouldn't spring things like that on me first thing in the morning."

"It means the same whatever time of day I tell you," she said, her irritation showing. "You could at least sound pleased for me."

Ben knew he'd responded negatively and hated himself for it. "I'm sorry, sweetheart. I am pleased for you, of course I am. How about we come to see you this weekend? We'll fly to Heathrow and pick up a hire car. Driving to Henley is easy so we should be with you by lunchtime.

"That's fine. It *will* be easy for you. We'll meet you in Henley for lunch. Give us a call when you're leaving Heathrow," she told him.

Eighteen

When Saturday came, Kim was on edge. "I'm dreading this," she disclosed to Simon. "I have a weird feeling something dreadful is going to happen."

"I wish I could say something to help," Simon told her. "I'm completely outside of this situation, baby. I haven't even met your parents yet, so I'm not in a position to pass an opinion one way or the other. I'll be here to support you whatever happens, but don't try to anticipate what it might be."

"I know you are right, but there's something going on. I've had this feeling for months. But for you, I think I would have gone mad."

Kim and Simon arrived early at the restaurant in Henley. When her mobile rang, she jumped nervously. "Hi, Mum. Are you on your way?" she asked as cheerfully as she was able.

"Your dad took the wrong exit from the motorway, but we're about ten minutes away now. We'll see you soon."

Kimberley smiled at Simon. "That was Mum. She actually sounded friendly. Maybe she's forgiven me for whatever I'd done wrong."

"I'm sure she has. Who could stay mad at you for more than two minutes?"

"That's your biased opinion again, but I'll take it," she said, happier now that she and her mother had at least exchanged a few friendly words.

Belinda and Ben arrived as arranged. Introductions over, they took a table in the bay window overlooking the river. "This is nice," Belinda commented. "Have you been here before?"

Kim noted that her mother was being particularly polite and precise. "I have," she said, "but as Simon has never been to England, he is being treated to it for the first time, as you are."

"How have you found London so far?" Ben asked. "Is it as busy as Sydney?"

"It's different, but I think both cities are busy in their own way. I still have to do the tourist bit. Kim hasn't had time yet to show me around properly," Simon told them.

Belinda smiled. "Kim never has time for anything. She is always busy."

"I know that already," Simon confirmed. "We both have extremely demanding jobs; demanding of time and commitment. That's why we make such a good couple."

"Oh goodness me," Belinda exclaimed. "How rude of me. Congratulations!"

"Thank you, Mrs Mason. I love Kimberley very much."

Belinda moved uncomfortably in her seat and Kim noticed. "Please call me Belinda. Mrs Mason seems so formal."

"Thank you so much, Mum," Kim said with exaggerated politeness. "Would you like to see my ring?" And she thrust out her left hand, giving Belinda no choice.

"Of course...it's beautiful. Did you choose it yourself?"

Kim smiled proudly at her fiancé. "All Simon's own work. It was a complete surprise and very unexpected, so that made it all the more special."

"I'm pleased for you," Belinda said as she stood up to hug them both.

Lunch was certainly pleasant enough after that and the conversation, in spite of few quiet moments, flowed reasonably well. Any little awkward silences that occurred were diffused with snippets of information about Kim's childhood from Ben. "Do you know, Simon, that Kim once ate the cat's food at her grandma's house? She was about two years old and Belinda's mother had a cat."

Kim laughed. "I remember that cat. He was the most majestic cat I've ever seen, but his food tasted like sh…"

"Kimberley!" her mother chastised.

"Sorry, Mum. My vocabulary isn't usually so graphic, but I can't think of any other way to describe the taste, not that I've ever tasted shit."

They all laughed; genuinely laughed; even Belinda managed a little smile.

"Trust you to lower the tone, Kimberley Mason," her dad said light-heartedly, "and at the lunch table too."

After lunch, they walked along the river and watched the boat crews being put through their paces. "Let's go back to Willow Bank and we'll have tea on the terrace. How English is that?" Kim asked them collectively.

"Very English," Ben agreed.

"Is this just for me?" Simon asked.

"Just to show you how civilised we are," Kim told him as she squeezed his hand affectionately.

"Very refined," Belinda commented. "It seems we did something right in your upbringing."

She stopped abruptly as Ben nudged her pointedly and then jumped in quickly.

"We'll follow you, Kim. Who's driving?"

"I am," Kim said. "Even though they drive on the left in Australia, Simon doesn't know the English roads yet, especially the little country lanes on the way to Willow Bank."

~ * ~

Ben was waiting for the right moment. They'd had tea; the evening sun was lending a balmy atmosphere to the terrace overlooking the Thames. The four people were seemingly in relaxed mood.

Ben began. "Do you consider you had an idyllic childhood, Kim?" he asked.

Kim stiffened. *Here it comes,* she thought nervously. "I would say I had a wonderful childhood. Why do you ask?" *Might as well get it over with, whatever it might be.*

Ben stood up as if he were about to deliver an oration, but his slow pacing of the floor told the others that he was nervous too. His outward appearance, however, displayed a man in control. "Your mum and I have deliberated long and hard about this," he said. "It isn't going to be easy for any of us..."

Kim breathed in deeply. "I know something is wrong," she told him. "I've known for weeks; months even. I haven't any idea what it is, but anything that can estrange me from my mother—and that's what it has felt like—anything that causes alienation from my parents, must be pretty bad." She moved closer to Simon and held tightly on to his hand.

"Please, Kim, let me continue," Ben pleaded. "It is important that your mum and I know at this point if you considered your childhood was lacking in any way."

Kim shook her head to acknowledge again that she had indeed experienced a wonderful childhood.

While Belinda looked down at her clasped hands on her lap, Ben continued earnestly. "Please tell me, Kim, if you think I've been a good father. I need to know..."

"What is this, Dad?" she interrupted. "You are the best dad I could ever have wished for. I've told you often enough, but where is all this leading?" She was becoming agitated. "Are you and Mum splitting up?"

Ben's eyes filled with tears. "No," he said, his voice trembling, "but we have something to tell you that perhaps we ought to have told you years ago." He related all the details of Belinda's dalliance with Joel Winston; her long term guilt and their decision to put Ben's name on the birth certificate. "I loved your mum then and I love her now."

Kim listened in stunned silence. Her heart was beating wildly in her chest, but when she spoke, her voice was strong and her manner confident. "You are not my father?" she asked, not waiting for an answer. "How could you do that to me, Dad? You have deliberately deceived me for almost thirty years. I can't believe you would do that to me. You above of all people." She paused while she breathed deeply in an effort to calm herself. "How many other lies have you told along the way?"

"We honestly thought we were doing what was right..."

"Right for whom?" she demanded jumping up from her seat and facing him challengingly. "Right for you; right for her..." She spat the words in her mother's direction. "What about me?"

Belinda looked at her daughter through tears of regret. "We know what we have done, Kim, and we are sorry."

"Sorry? Sorry?" Kim ranted. "Sorry for what? Sorry that you were easy enough to allow some guy to get into your knickers before you were married? Sorry you weren't honest enough to accept what you'd done? Sorry you lied to your parents, to your family and friends and most of all, sorry you lied to *me*? Give me a break, Mother. You're sorry you've had to come clean thirty years on."

Belinda didn't have a suitable answer that would pacify Kim.

Kim sighed deeply. She was shocked and it showed. "I hope you *do* realise what you have done," she said pointedly. "I see now why there was such consternation about my going to Australia. Joel Winston meant absolutely nothing to me except that my prospective father-in-law said I had his colouring." She raised her arms sideways and let them fall heavily in frustration. "No bloody wonder I have his colouring!" she exclaimed.

Simon placed his arm around Kim shoulders. "Maybe I should leave you guys to talk," he said gently. "I'll go for a walk along the river. These long English summer nights are perfect for that. I'll be back shortly, Kim. You need to talk to your parents alone."

"No, you don't need to do that, darl," she told him. "I would like you to be here with me. I need your love and support. God knows, at the moment there's very little coming from the two people whose unconditional love and support I thought I'd had all my life. How wrong could I have been?"

"That's not fair, Kimberley," Ben interrupted. "We have always been there for you."

"That was your conscience, Da..." She paused poignantly. "I guess I call you Ben now," she said scathingly.

Belinda gasped. Ben shuddered. "That's pretty much below the belt, Kim. I have to tell you that on my insistence Joel agreed never to acknowledge his part in all this. I told him to keep the hell away from us and promise never to have anything to do with you. He has kept his promise and I have to respect him for that," he said.

"How come we went to Australia for his wedding then? It *was* his wedding we went to, wasn't it?" Kim asked, suddenly realising how the pieces of the jigsaw fit together. "I understand now why that trip has never been discussed in the Mason household, but why on earth did we go all that way for *his* wedding?"

"We made our peace of sorts when we bought their house."

Kim gasped. "This gets worse. Are you telling me I have been brought up in Joel Winston's house? Bloody hell!"

"Well yes, but that was never an issue. We liked the house; they were selling so we bought it. Simple as that. I have to say we thought going to Perth for the wedding would help clarify things for us all. We decided we would go as a family unit to emphasise our togetherness to them. At the time that was important for us to show how strong we were. Mrs Winston, too, said she would always acknowledge you as our daughter; she made that clear from the start. She had a lot of baggage of her own to sort out and she invited us out there on an all-expenses paid trip to gather Joel's friends together as a surprise on his big day. I guess it eased her conscience for what she'd done in the past." Ben didn't know how much of the Winston history was relevant to Kim. "We have to admit, we grasped the opportunity to travel to Australia as the trip of a lifetime. Then we decided we would never refer to it when we returned so Joel wouldn't be a part of our lives ever again."

"You continue to astound me," Kim said. "How naïve can you be? Just seeing me must have been a constant reminder of him every day. Well, I take my hat off to your acting abilities, both of you."

"We didn't look at it as an act, Kim," Belinda added, gaining a little confidence to add to the discussion. "I loved you as *my* daughter, not as Joel's. Your dad..." She paused deliberately and sighed. "Ben has been more of a father to you than Joel would ever have been. I can safely say that and Penny and Gerry would agree."

"Are you saying that Auntie Penny and Uncle Gerry know about all this?" Kim asked incredulously.

Belinda went quiet again and allowed Ben to answer the questions. "They do and they have been the most loyal and trustworthy friends we could ever have wished for, to us and to Joel, too as it happens. Gerry is very close to Joel and although he never approved of what he did, their friendship withstood the test of time. He still writes and talks to Joel regularly, but I understand that your name is never mentioned between them."

"Like I don't matter? Is that it?" Kim spat. "The man I thought was my father has lied to me for thirty years and the man who is my father pretends I don't exist."

Ben was distraught. "Of course you matter, Kim. Can't you at least try to understand that we kept all this from you to protect you? I loved you as my own child; I still love you. I am your father in every respect except that you don't have my DNA."

"I accept that you have always been a good and loving father. It would be very wrong of me to do otherwise, but I can't get past the thought of your deceit, your lies, your idea that not telling the truth was the right thing to do," she said. "I trusted you with my life and you abused that trust. I'm not sure I can ever forgive you for that," she cried as the tears of sadness filled her eyes. "And you, Mother; I am allowed to call you that, because you gave birth to me, but in addition to your lies, I hate the underhanded way you constantly tried to put obstacles in my way as regards my work in Australia, not to mention your objection to Simon before you even met him and that fills me with contempt. Now I realise it was all done as a selfish attempt to cover up your teenage promiscuity, of which I presume you are now ashamed." She leaned on the wrought iron railings thinking that their coldness just about described her relationship with the two people behind her. Turning to face them again, she asked, "And what does Tony know of this?"

Ben answered quickly before Kim aimed more of her tirade at them. "He knows nothing apart from the fact that something is wrong between us. Life at home has not been easy for the past few months. He spends a lot of time with Liz renovating their new house for when they get married."

"Good for him," Kim said and then with realisation, "Aha, now I see why he was the blue-eyed boy for living at home instead of shacking up with Liz. You made that pretty clear all along that you loved him for not living with Liz before his marriage and you also made it clear that you disapproved of my sleeping arrangements. Your sins will find you out, hey Mother?"

Belinda stared at the floor. She couldn't look her daughter in the eye and her tears were preventing her from seeing clearly.

Ben was clutching at straws. "How were we to know your job would take you back to Australia, or that you would link up with a family who knows Joel? The whole situation is bizarre."

"And whose fault is that?" Kim asked with venom in her voice. She looked past them and spoke to Simon. "Please, Simon, let's go for that walk. I need some space away from these people."

Nineteen

In Perth, Western Australia, Joel and Sheralyn Winston were still reeling from the revelations the television show *Performing for Australia* had brought to light. "That really has put the cat among the pigeons," Joel said. "How on earth can I work for the Obertelli Agency when Kimberley Mason has such connections with it?"

Sheralyn, ever the pragmatist, thought about the situation before she spoke. "Look, Joel," she said pointedly. "As far as we're concerned, Kimberley Mason knows nothing about you. It can be reasonably assumed that your paths will never cross. How often will you have to go to Sydney, or will she have to come to Perth?"

"I don't know," Joel admitted. "There might be occasions when we have to be in the same place..." He shrugged questioningly.

Sheralyn continued. "My view is that we leave well enough alone. How can they possibly know we saw her on TV? We have never broken our promise to the Masons. They must know that.

They don't know that you will be working for OTA unless Gerry has told them. Do you think that's a possibility?" She looked at Joel through enquiring eyes.

"I haven't told Gerry yet and with what's happened now, perhaps I won't tell him at all, although what would they know about the Obertellis? We never mention Kimberley. The only way I was able to do that was to block all thoughts of Ben and Belinda and forget what happened thirty years ago. Sher, you have to believe me. You and our kids are the most important people in my life."

Sheralyn took his hand in hers to reassure him. "I know that, babe. Everybody has a past they would prefer to forget. We dealt with yours before we got married; we'll deal with this too. Don't worry."

"From my own point of view," Joel continued, "they stopped communicating with me years ago; not even a Christmas card these days, so I guess they have blocked me from their minds too." He paused to gather his thoughts. "About the job, though...I really want the change of direction. I need it, but it isn't going to be easy. Shane Obertelli has already commented about the likeness."

"He's what?" Sheralyn was flabbergasted.

"Oh that's typical of Shane. He was joking, of course, but he told me to warn you before people started casting aspersions," he explained. "He really has no idea there is any connection whatsoever and thank God for that."

"Ah well, babe, let's just play it by ear," Sheralyn suggested. "I still think we have to carry on as normal. We'll deal with whatever happens, if and when."

~ * ~

Simon and Kim walked hand in hand along the riverbank. It was quiet and peaceful, in sharp contrast to the tumult they had left behind at the house. Not a lot was discussed until Kim suddenly announced, "I'll wind up Premier Plus and come to live permanently in Sydney."

"What are you talking about, Kim?" Simon asked, concern etched all over his face.

"My life here ended today. How do you think I feel about that?" she asked pointedly.

Simon stopped in his tracks. He placed his hands on Kim's shoulders and looked directly into her eyes. "This is a knee-jerk reaction, Kim. Please don't make hasty decisions."

"Are you telling me you don't want me in Sydney?" she asked, tears welling up in her dark eyes.

"No, of course not, but you are in shock...I'm in shock..."

"Shock doesn't come anywhere near to how I feel." Her voice was weak and trembling. "I spent almost thirty years thinking I had the perfect family. I had a mother who cared for me and was my best friend, a dad who was the best in the world, a brother who was the proverbial pain in the backside, but was always there for me," she explained. "In the past half hour, my world has been completely smashed to smithereens."

"I don't know what to say, babe," Simon told her. "I can't imagine what is going on inside your head, but I want you to know I love you. I'm here for you and whatever you decide to do, I'll support you every step of the way."

Kim looked directly into Simon's eyes. "Do I really look like Joel Winston?" she asked.

Simon smiled affectionately. "Yes, I'm afraid you do," he conceded. "There must be millions of young Australian women who'd all give their eye teeth to be the daughter of Joel Winston and here you are, not knowing how to cope with the revelation that you really are his daughter."

"What do I do, Simon?" she asked dolefully.

Simon held her close to him. "You do nothing until you have come to terms with what you have just found out," he advised. "We'll talk about it tomorrow when the dust has settled a bit. In the meantime, we had better go back and see how we make your relationship with your parents more bearable."

When they arrived back at the house, it was in darkness and her parents' car had gone. Kim found a letter on the kitchen table.

Dearest Kim,

We know you are hurting right now and we wish we could do something to ease your pain. We know also that your whole world has been turned upside down and we shall be eternally sorry for doing that to you. We don't wish to make excuses for our actions, but there are a couple of things you should know before you make any decisions. First of all, no parents could have loved their child more than we loved you as you were growing up. As your dad, I felt every attachment any father would proudly associate with the birth of his first child. You have to believe that.

Secondly, your mum has lived with the guilt of her flirtation with Joel Winston throughout your life. After our trip to Australia, blocking out all thoughts of him and severing all links was the only way we were able to lead normal lives, or at least what passed for normal. Your recent links to Australia opened up old wounds and caused your mum to become completely distraught, thinking that somehow you would bump into Joel and her past would come to light. The fact that we had kept it secret made the situation much worse.

We cannot blame any of this on Joel Winston. We didn't like what he did, but he was always honest about the situation and he has kept his promise to acknowledge you as my daughter. I have to respect him for that. At this point, we don't know what the implications will be as regards your links with the Obertelli Agency. It is clear that Simon's father knows Joel and saw the resemblance in your features. Hopefully it was just a passing observation. We don't know how Mr Obertelli knew him in the first place, but Joel has a wife and family of his own now and may not wish you to intrude in that. The whole situation needs to be thought about carefully. Too many lives will be affected if…well, I just can't think about it at the moment.

We feel it best that we don't stay in your home tonight. There is and will be too much tension between us and we think you and Simon need your space.

On a much more pleasant note, we like Simon and know he will be a wonderful husband for you. Be happy, both of you. That's all we ask.

All our love as always,
Mum and Dad xx

Kim gently placed the letter on the table and hot tears coursed down her cheeks. Simon went to put his arms around her and she clung to him like a frightened child.

~ * ~

Ben and Belinda drove straight to the airport and managed to obtain two seats on the last shuttle to Manchester that night. By midnight, they were back in Bolton. Few words had been spoken during the journey, but Belinda had held on tightly to Ben's hand, at times until her knuckles were white. Ben was the first to speak.

"We have to tell Tony what is going on. He has to know. How he'll react is anybody's guess. I actually think he'll be there for his sister, but not for us."

Belinda looked at him with wide eyes. "He won't care about us. Now he's started staying with Liz at the weekends, he's lost a lot of my respect. Why should we worry too much about Tony? He's taking Kim's lead and sleeping with his girlfriend before he's married," she said, still with an air of self-pity.

"And whose fault is that, Bel?" Ben asked, not quite believing what he was hearing. "This house has been like a morgue the past few weeks and we've ignored his questions when he asked what was wrong. We've driven him into the arms of Liz. To be honest, I'm happy for him. I would hope you would be, too and it might help you to lighten up about modern day relationships after all this. You can't punish everybody because of what happened to you. Tony is our son—yours and mine, the one thing we made together. I'd like you to remember that."

"What have we done, Ben? We are going to lose both our children through our mishandling of this inescapable situation. I regret the whole damned business," Belinda said resignedly.

"Don't talk like that," Ben answered forcefully. "We'll have to live through it. We'll deal with Tony when we have to, but Kim will work it out eventually. She is sensitive enough to see the whole picture once she's calmed down."

"She's also strong-willed and more than a little self-righteous," Belinda stated categorically, "and given the present circumstances, she'll use that to her advantage. I know she will. We can't get away from those Winston characteristics, however much we try."

Ben sighed, a long, deep and meaningful expulsion of breath to express his growing exasperation. "Bel, you have to stop blaming Joel. He was honest with you from the outset. You can't deny that and we made demands of him afterwards that he has always respected to the letter. We gave him no choice in the matter."

"That's easy for you to say, Ben."

"Easy? I don't think so," Ben interrupted. "I took on you and his child when I was eighteen years old. I knew you didn't love me then and I'm not sure you love me now. Just recently I have felt a rejection I thought I would never again experience."

Belinda gasped. "I haven't rejected you, Ben. You can't possibly feel that way," she cried. "How on earth can you say that?"

"I can say it because it's true and don't try to tell me how I feel, Bel. Until you have spent twenty-nine years knowing that you were second best, you cannot understand what it's like, nor have an opinion on it." Ben was releasing all the tensions of years gone by. He was trembling inside, but his voice was strong. "I have said this many times before, but it seems you haven't listened. I loved you then; I love you now, but God knows you make it very difficult at times. The past few weeks have been purgatory for me knowing you have been harking back to that one reckless afternoon in the attic room at the Connollys' shop."

Belinda stood up and moved aggressively towards her husband. "Go on, Ben," she snarled, throwing her arms in the air in mounting rage. "Rub it in a bit more. You seem to delight in that."

"No, you're wrong, Bel. You have no idea what it's like to see the longing in your eyes even when you are castigating Joel for how he treated you. And while we are baring all, I heard you singing when you were sorting out the stuff in the attic and I also heard what you said afterwards. Don't tell me those weren't words of regret, because I will never believe you."

"Yes, they were words of regret, but not in the way you think," she said harshly.

"What do I think, Belinda? What exactly do I think?"

"You think this is all about you and what a hero you were to marry me," she told him bitterly. "You think I have lied about loving you for all these years; you think..."

Ben stared at the woman he had rescued from the brink of despair all those years ago and couldn't comprehend what she was saying now. "Don't tempt me, Belinda," he said calmly. "I don't know you anymore. How vicious can you be? A few moments ago, I said I still loved you. Well, I'm not so sure about that now."

"Aha, now the truth comes out," she said boldly. "Don't worry about me, Ben Mason. I'm just the person who has had to suffer the humiliation of being used by a supercilious teenager who thought he was better than me and now by the man who has pretended to love me unconditionally for twenty-nine years."

Ben was dumbfounded. "And *you* have the audacity to call Kimberley arrogant and self-possessed," Ben said blatantly. "Well, no wonder she's like that with you for a mother!" He looked at the clock. It was two o'clock in the morning. "I've heard enough. I'm going to bed. I'll sleep in Kim's room and you may read into that whatever you like. I'm past caring."

~ * ~

Ben didn't sleep soundly. His thoughts were full of what had been said between him and his wife. The words, *I'm not sure I love you anymore* went over and over in his mind. He began to question his feelings. *I'm devastated. There is no other word for it. I have loved Belinda since I first saw her and now I find myself questioning that love. It's true I don't like her very much at the moment. She is only thinking of herself; not of Kim; not of Tony; not of me. But I can't believe she thinks I considered myself a hero in marrying her. Do I really feel like that?* He shifted restlessly in the unfamiliar bed. *I loved her. I wasn't playing at being a hero; of course I wasn't. I would have done anything for her and she knew it.* He felt the tears trickle down his cheeks. His heart was beating strongly in his chest and he felt his anger rising like it used to when he lay in his bed as a child covering his ears to block out the obnoxious grunts and groans coming from the deadbeats his mother brought home each night. *I escaped all that,* he thought angrily. *I thought I'd made up for all the rubbish my parents laid on me as I was growing up. I wanted so much better for my wife, my kids and for me and God knows, I made it. I know I made it. I'm proud of myself for that and I'm proud of the way I have treated Belinda and our children.* He breathed in deeply again. *Is that arrogance? I don't think so.* He drifted off into a fitful sleep. His dreams were full of his little princess Kimberley whom he adored with all his heart, but she was screaming at him like a banshee and telling him to get away from her. Belinda joined in, "Who's the hero now, Benny boy?" but it was Joel Winston's voice and all the time, Tony crouched in a corner covering his ears. He woke with a start, sweating, his breathing fast, his heart palpitating in his chest and still myriads of unhappy thoughts invaded his brain.

~ * ~

Belinda stared through the darkness, seeing nothing, but desperately trying to work out where she had to go from here. *Is this all my fault?* she silently asked herself. *Do I really have to take all the blame for this ridiculous state of affairs?* In a moment of contrition, she admitted her wrong-doing. *I guess I should be willing to accept the responsibility and face up to my own indiscretions. I can't blame Ben for that. He has done everything he could to make my life happy. Why did I throw it all back in his face?* She sat up and plumped up her pillows to make herself comfortable. *Ben really has been a good father to Kim, but I still think her attitude is down to Joel, not me. She has his looks, his swagger, his talent...* She smiled to herself, albeit only a half-smile. *No wonder I fell for him,* she mused. *I had never seen anybody so good looking. How could I ever forget that day at the Café Bellissimo...*

~ * ~

"Well, look who it is," she said as he found a table near the window.

"Excuse me," Joel said, noting that there was a guitar resting against the chair next to the louder of the two girls, "but do I know you?"

"Not really, but I know you," she told him. "You weren't very polite when you were on the train last week. I had to squeeze between you and an old man reading a newspaper and I had to ask you to move your feet. A girl shouldn't have to ask for a seat. A gentleman would have offered her one."

"I'm sorry I gave you that impression," he said. "I'm not usually bad mannered. My mother would be disgusted if she thought I'd mistreated a lady," he joked, realising that his mother would indeed be aghast at his attitude, "but since she's not here, I'll make amends before she finds out. Can I buy you another coffee?"

"What do you think, Penny? Shall we let a stranger buy us a drink?"

Penny smiled shyly and nodded. "Okay," she said quietly, almost cowering behind her large coffee mug. "Cappuccino, please."

"Is that two cappuccinos then?" Joel asked.

"Thanks," she replied, "I don't mind if I do."

Joel went to the counter, ordered three cappuccinos and returned to the table in the window. "Do you mind if I join you? I'm Joel.

"Oooh, that's a po..."

"... posh name?" Joel asked.

"How did you know what I was going to say? Are you psychic or something?" the girl asked.

"Sort of," Joel replied. "You must be the sixth or seventh person to say that in the past week."

"Well, it does sound a bit posh. I'm Belinda and she's Penny."

"And you're saying my name's posh! Belinda and Penelope..."

"Oh, don't call me that," Penny cried, suddenly becoming animated. "I hate it. Penny's bad enough and I've even been called ha'penny by my dad when I was little, but Penelope! God knows where my mum found that name."

Joel grinned. "Okay, let's call a truce. Discussion of names forbidden in any future conversations. Agreed?

"So we're going to have future conversations, are we?" Belinda asked.

~ * ~

Still smiling, she drew up her knees and hugged them to her. *I guess we had a bit more than a conversation,* she thought. *I wish I'd never met him. More to the point, I wish I hadn't let him near me, but I did and God, have I had to live with the consequences?* She shrugged as if in willing acceptance of the situation. *I could never have anticipated that thirty years on, I would be contemplating my future because of him? Damn you, Joel Winston.* She sighed sadly. *Kim hates me; Ben hates me; Tony will probably hate me when he finds out.* She shivered involuntarily and snuggled back under the duvet. *Maybe I'll go to Penny's for a few days. She has stood by me through all this and Ben and I need our space just now. God knows I need some friendly support at the moment.* She closed her eyes and eventually drifted off to sleep.

Twenty

Simon had to return to Sydney after Kim's estrangement from her parents to ensure his business was functioning as he required. "I'll be back in three months," he told Kim as he left Heathrow. "When I return, we'll make our plans and tie up loose ends here. I love you. Always remember that."

"I know that, baby," she replied with great affection. "I love you too."

"You don't have to sell Premier Plus, you know," he told her for the umpteenth time in the last few weeks.

"Yes I do. I've made up my mind, Simon. I've done all I want to do here. Melissa and Gary are becoming joint owners and continuing their affiliation with us at the Obertelli Agency in Sydney. That's one of the conditions of sale. We'll still be in regular contact with them and don't forget, I'm keeping my Chelsea flat for when we come back to the UK."

"I just want you to be sure you are doing what is right for you Kim; not for Melissa; not for Gary; not for me, but for you."

Kim looked at the man who had become her friend, her lover and her soul mate in such a short space of time. "This is right for me, darl. Believe me, I know what I'm doing," and with that she sadly waved Simon off as he went through passport control on his way back home, this time knowing he would definitely be back.

~ * ~

Kim and Simon married with a quiet ceremony at Chelsea Register Office in January 1996. Melissa and Gary were their witnesses and no other guests were invited. They had lunch at The Ivy and as Melissa and Gary went back to the office, Kim and Simon returned to the Chelsea flat.

"You know," she said cheerily, "With Willow Bank sold and Premier Plus continuing under the direction of the new owners, I feel wonderfully liberated."

"Good on yer!" her husband replied and he smiled lovingly at his new wife. Once they were alone in the flat, he hugged her and whispered in her ear, "You look absolutely divine, Mrs. Obertelli, and you have made me a very happy man."

Kim placed her arms around his neck and drew him close. "I'm very happy too," she murmured as she nuzzled his neck.

"Are you, Kim? Are you really happy?"

"Of course I am. Why wouldn't I be?"

Simon led her to the settee and they both sat. Kim was looking at him closely, trying to see some hint of what he intended to say. "What is this?" she asked tentatively.

Simon spoke quietly and with sensitivity. "Today we got married. It is reputed to be the most wonderful day in a woman's life; the day when she should be surrounded by her family and friends."

"Oh I see," she offered knowingly.

"Would you like to let your family know we are married?" he asked gently.

"I don't think so."

"I'm sure they would want to know," Simon continued.

Kim sighed. "I understand what you are saying, darl, and maybe they would want to know, but I can't forgive them yet and it would be hypocritical for me to call when I am so happy. They haven't made contact with me for almost a year and when Tony called soon after the big revelation, he made it very clear he was on their side. He told me to get over it, or get out. I thought that was pretty mean. I can't believe he hasn't tried to see my point of view, but then when you think about it, *he* is their son..." She paused poignantly. "They made *him* together."

"Sweetheart, I'm sorry. This is our day and I've made you unhappy. Forgive me, please."

"Nothing to forgive. I'd be lying if I said I hadn't thought about them today, but I refuse to allow them to spoil my happiness. Now I have a very special wedding present for you."

Simon looked at her disapprovingly. "I thought we agreed not to buy presents for each other until we have the church blessing when we are back in Sydney," he said. "I've been very tempted to buy something for you, but I didn't think you'd go back on our agreement so I didn't bother."

"I know, sweetheart, and I'm sorry, but I couldn't resist this," she said with her most disarming smile. "I'm pregnant."

Simon scooped her up in his arms and carried her to their bed. "A baby!" he exclaimed, "Just what I wanted!" and he grinned ecstatically. Suddenly he went quiet before he asked, "Does that mean we can't consummate our marriage?"

"Of course not," she assured him. "I made sure of that when I saw the doctor. No problemo."

~ * ~

On the same day as the wedding in London, but later than anticipated, the Obertelli Theatrical Agency in Perth officially opened its doors with a champagne reception at the new offices in

Northbridge. The location was perfect for Joel and on a good day he would be able to drive to work in fifteen minutes.

"Here we go at last," he said to Sheralyn as he left for work on the first day. "Who'd have thought it would have taken so long to refurbish the new premises? Wish me luck, darl."

"I do wish you luck, or should I say break a leg?" she asked cheerily. "Enjoy it, babe, and no need to worry about the problems arising from *Performing for Australia*. They seem to have disappeared now the series is over."

"I agree," Joel replied confidently. "Nobody has latched on to the likeness, not even our own kids, so I'm happy about that. Gerry hasn't mentioned anything about her as usual, so I guess they are all in the dark over there."

Sheralyn smiled at her husband. "You know, Joel," she said quietly. "I am so proud of the way you have handled all this. We can't dwell on the past; it happened and we can't change it. The Masons are obviously happy with the way things are and we wouldn't want to do anything to upset their lives. Just go and do a good job, darl. I'll see you later. Love you."

"Love you too. See you when I see you!" he quipped.

"What's that supposed to mean?"

"It means I have no idea what time I'll be home. I'll have to settle into my new office and make a start on implementing my plans. I have three new staff to consider and I'm not sure if they know the ropes. Shane is sending me a girl from Sydney who has worked at OTA before, but she doesn't arrive until next week."

~ * ~

The first week flew by and Joel began to establish contacts straight away. He had two talent scouts who visited the local amateur theatres and stage schools and who reported back daily with prospective clients for Joel to audition. Links with Sydney and Melbourne were already in place and there would be an exchange of artistes on a regular basis. *Eventually*, Joel thought, *the UK exchange programme will take off as well and I'm very excited about that.*

When Joel arrived at the office to begin his second week, he was greeted by a young woman waiting in Reception. "Good morning," he said. "You are early. What can I do for you?"

"Shane Obertelli sent me," she told him.

"Oh my goodness! I'm so sorry," Joel apologised. "I'm Joel Winston."

"I know," she replied with a beaming smile. "I used to be so madly in love with you! I watched every single series of *Have You Got What It Takes?* and the spin-offs," she told him excitedly.

"Well, you obviously enjoyed it," he commented, "Miss...? Sorry, I don't know your name."

The girl looked at him confidently. "Grainger—but call me Janine."

"Good to meet you, Janine," Joel told her. "I believe you know the ropes at OTA in Sydney."

"I do, but I don't work there anymore," she explained. "I work for James Radicchio, but Shane Obertelli sort of borrowed me back to come over here to help you for a couple of weeks. Simon Obertelli is in the UK at the moment and his father is in charge in his absence."

"Oh I see," Joel replied. "Does he travel to the UK often?"

"I don't know," she said. "I have nothing to do with him these days." She paused briefly and then a look of realisation spread across her face. "You have just broken a dream, so to speak."

"A good one, I hope."

"Well, weird really. You'll never believe this, but when Kimberley Mason...you know the woman who was on *Performing for Australia?*...when she came into the Sydney office, I knew she reminded me of somebody and now I know who it is. It's YOU!"

"You're right; I don't believe it," Joel said quickly, hoping that what he was feeling inside didn't show on the outside. "Shall we get started? I'll show you what we've done so far.

~ * ~

"How are you, Poshman?" Gerry asked when he called Joel a few weeks after OTA Perth had opened.

"Wacker! Great to hear from you," Joel exclaimed. "It's been ages."

"I know, but it's good to talk to you. How're things?" his Liverpudlian friend asked.

"Not three bad…"

"Hey that's my line," Gerry broke in. "Posh boys like you don't say silly things like that."

"They do now, Wacker. Being friends with you for twenty odd years, well it kind of rubs off. Seriously though, how are Penny and Maggie? And what are the boys doing these days?" Joel asked.

"They're all good. Mam's moved into a granny flat next to our Chrissie's. She sold the shop after our dad died. She'll cope, though. After all, our ol' man wasn't home that often. I think he had two wives; our mam and the Dublin ferry boat!" Gerry told him.

Joel had to laugh. "I wish I could view life like you, Wack. It sure does make our trials and tribulations seem easier to cope with."

"I don't believe in being miserable; never did; never shall. I'll tell you about my boys in a minute, but tell me what's happening down under," Gerry continued with typical enthusiasm in his voice.

"Life is great. I'm not performing anymore, but I've taken on a new role," Joel told him eagerly. "Sheralyn kept telling me I was becoming an old rocker and you know me, I couldn't allow my image to slip. Being a grey-haired pop star just doesn't do it for me."

"Same old Winston," Gerry quipped. "What are you doing now? You'll already have made your millions, so money won't matter."

"In your dreams, Connolly! I wish!" Joel said cheerily. "I'm running a theatrical agency in Perth. It's a new branch of the Obertelli Agency based in Sydney. It was Shane Obertelli who brought me out to Australia in the first place." *Damn,* he thought as soon as the words were out of his mouth. *I didn't intend to say anything about that to Gerry. Oh dear!*

Gerry went quiet.

"Are you still there, Wack?" Joel asked.

It took Gerry a few seconds to answer. "I'm still here. I think you've just opened a can of worms," he said in his usual honest manner.

Now it was Joel's turn to go quiet, but taking a sharp intake of breath, he answered, "Have I? Why?"

"Can I be honest, Joel?"

"When haven't you been honest with me, Wacker?" Joel continued, "And if you're calling me Joel, it must be pretty serious. Just tell me. I'm ready for it."

Joel heard Gerry taking in a deep breath too before he began. "Ben and Belinda have split up.

"You're joking," Joel exclaimed. "Am I allowed to ask why?"

"I don't know how much of this you will know, seeing that you have just disclosed that you're working for the Obertelli Agency."

"I don't know anything really; only that Kimberley Mason is involved with the agency in Sydney. She did a couple of TV appearances over here a while ago. I left well alone, because it's unlikely our paths will cross and nobody over here knows anything about the situation other than Sheralyn and me and Mum and Sean," Joel explained. "I can assure you, we have never gone back on the promise we made to them and Ben and I stopped communicating years ago. I just assumed they thought it was easier that way. We all had to get on with our lives."

"To a point, that's exactly what they thought, too. Strange though it may seem, they never talked about you after the wedding. Belinda didn't want Kim to hear your name—not ever.

She was quite paranoid about it. When we were with them, your name never cropped up once in all those years. We all sort of accepted that was the way it had to be," Gerry expounded.

"That's fair enough. We did the same here in a way. We didn't talk about the Masons until just recently when Kim was on TV. It was a bit of a shock to us all, I can tell you. Mum was hell bent on contacting her...you know what my mother's like...but we joined forces, that is, Sean, Sher and me...to stop her interfering. We had to assume Kimberley knew nothing about me. We still think that..." He paused pointedly. "...unless you are saying otherwise now, in which case, bloody hell fire, Wacker!"

"Are you sitting down, mate?" Gerry asked him.

"Yes, as it happens, I am and thank God I'm alone. The rest of the family is out for the day...there's a rally in King's Park, something to do with university fees. I had some paper work to catch up on so Sher has gone along with the kids; there's a barbecue afterwards," Joel told him. "Now tell me what I need to know."

Gerry started at the beginning, leaving out Joel's fleeting flirtation with the drug culture in the 60s. He explained how they had all lied to Belinda's parents and anybody else who knew her, how Penny and Gerry had been sworn to secrecy and how they had continued their loyalty to their friends all the years since then. "It was only when Kim got involved with the Obertellis that Belinda started becoming paranoid. The Australian connection uprooted the past and she couldn't handle it. They decided to come clean with Kim because Belinda threw a wobbler. She was convinced Kim would bump into you somewhere and you would recognise each other. I don't know if you realise how like you she is in looks and personality."

"I noticed and so have a few others; Shane Obertelli and one of his staff, but none of them are aware that we're connected. I just played it down when it was mentioned and thank God none of them pursued the issue. As regards meeting her, Australia's a big place, Wacker, you know that. The odds of us bumping into each other are pretty slim, especially when she lives in the UK and is only here intermittently."

"We all know that, but try convincing Belinda. Mate, I'm telling you, she just went doolally about it and made Ben's life a misery."

"But I thought she and Ben had got it together," Joel said. "There must have been something if they were together for thirty years. It doesn't make sense after all this time."

"Well, the balloon went up about a year ago. Ben did everything he could to try to stop Bel from worrying. I don't think I could have been so patient."

Joel sighed audibly. "That's Ben to a tee," he said. "He was always like that at school, down to earth and sensible beyond his years. I always admired his commitment in everything he did, but then again, he had to be like that. I realised that a long time ago."

Gerry continued. "They decided they owed it to Kim to tell her the truth, because Belinda was tired of living on the edge, so to speak. Kim was getting curious anyway, because Bel kept objecting to her trips to Australia and then when she and the Obertelli boy got engaged...well, you can imagine the uproar that caused."

"Bloody hell fire," Joel said again with feeling. "She's engaged to Simon Obertelli? My God!" His mind was racing. "I never thought they'd tell her the truth, though and I'm really sorry they've split up over it. I guess that puts me in a very dodgy situation. What do you think I should do, Wack?"

"I suggest you do nothing, for the time being anyway. Belinda came to us for a while and bent Penny's ear for a month or two, and in all honesty, we were glad to see the back of her when she left. It doesn't matter how close a friend she is, living with that sort of anger and desperation is very wearing. Pen deserves a royal accolade for how she coped. Bel blames you, of course, but nobody else does after all this time. We all know these things happen, but Belinda just couldn't let go of the guilt. Look, Poshman, none of us likes remembering the details, but it was a long time ago and Ben has said all through this unfortunate situation that you aren't to blame for the split. He blames Belinda and Belinda blames everybody except herself. She even told Ben to stop playing the hero for marrying her. There's no recovering when one side is so totally blinkered and unbending. She's back in the house and Ben has an apartment above the bank."

Joel was at a loss as to what to say, but tried to look at it sensibly. "Look Wack, I can't deny I was at the root of the problem to begin with. I was young, irresponsible and a complete tool and I shall be eternally sorry about that. Ben asked me to acknowledge Kim as his daughter and I have always done that. I don't want a medal or anything, but I really have honoured their wishes to the letter. I'm very lucky Sheralyn forgave me before we were married and as you know, we have three wonderful kids of our own. Look, it's nineteen ninety-six and views about relationships are different these days. Can't Belinda see that? My son Glenn has already announced he's moving in with his girlfriend, next week as a matter of fact. We're going along with it because he'll only have sex behind our backs if we don't and he's probably done it already anyway...once a Winston always a Winston, hey Wack?" he joked to relieve the tension.

"Oh mate, I know you've changed," Gerry said with understanding. "Let's face it, it's thirty years ago. We have all had to grow up, but I have to inform you, Kim does know you're her father."

Joel gasped audibly.

"Apparently she resents her parents for lying to her for thirty years and she resents you for not acknowledging her for the same length of time," Gerry continued. "I hope she understands why you didn't. She's a clever young woman and once she's thought about it, she'll figure it out. Don't worry, she hates Pen and me too for going along with all the lies. Poor kid, she must feel completely abandoned at the moment since Anthony has written her off too because she won't accept the situation with good grace."

"Well, I don't know what to say except thanks for letting me know, Wack," Joel said quietly. "In a strange sort of way, I appreciate it. I'll just have to deal with whatever happens when it happens. If you see Ben, please tell him I'm sorry and if he needs to talk, even if it's only to castigate me again, tell him I'm here. I'll take whatever he wants to throw at me and I mean that sincerely."

"I'll tell him, Poshman, but I doubt he'll want to have a go at you. Like I said, he doesn't blame you for the present situation," Gerry reiterated. "You have to believe that." He paused and released a deep sigh of relief. "Now I almost forgot why I called in the first place. Rob is getting married next month and would like to bring his new wife out to Australia. Jessica's a great girl, a lot like Penny. They'll be backpacking most of the time, but would like to catch up with you when they hit Perth. Is that okay?"

"Of course it's okay," Joel enthused. "I haven't seen Robert since he was a toddler shouting, 'Come on you Reds!' And I haven't met your Paul at all, so whenever *he* wants to backpack around Australia, give him my number. They could use Mum and Sean, too, as a Gold Coast base. Just let me know when."

"That's excellent, Poshman. Who knows? Maybe Pen and I will come over again too sometime."

"I'll hold you to that, Wacker," Joel told him, "but just before you go, do you think Kim will contact me when she's over here? And how much do I say if she does? Forewarned is forearmed, so to speak."

"I don't know about that, mate," Gerry informed him. "I do know she has been told everything and really, you are not the main issue here; she is. She's a nice kid, Poshman, with a modern concept of life in general. She and Belinda are like chalk and cheese. I don't think she'll be spoiling for a row with you. We'll speak again soon. Cheers, mate."

"Cheers, Wack and thanks. You're a good mate. The best." Joel replaced the receiver and went to his favourite seat on the deck to contemplate what he had just been told.

Twenty-one

Kim and Simon arrived in Sydney just after Easter 1996. They had organized Kim's temporary residency visa before they left the UK. They decided she wouldn't want to work for a while after she'd had the baby and the spouse visa enabled her to settle into her new life before the baby arrived in September.

"A spring *bambino*," Mama O enthused when she was told the news. "He will have beautiful spring weather where he can flourish like a new flower."

"He?" Simon asked, laughing at his loving mother's enthusiasm. "Another little *bambino* for you to spoil, hey Mama?"

"I'm allowed to spoil him," she said indignantly. "I'm his *nonna*."

"Well, so long as you don't interfere with what we want to do as parents, Mama," Simon told her, mindful of Kim's independence.

"I won't, *figlio mio*," she assured him, "but I'll love him like every *nonna* loves her *nipoti*. What about your parents, Kim? Will they come to visit soon?"

Kim looked sad. "Not anytime soon, Mama O."

Simon took over gently. "Mama, we can talk about that another time, but not now. Okay?"

"Of course okay," Mama O said cheerily and then more seriously, "Mama O *non deve immischiarsi.*" *Mama O mustn't interfere.*

Simon smiled. "Thank you, Mama."

Kim listened, fascinated, but wanted to change the subject. "I'll be speaking Italian soon," she said. "Already I have picked up a few words. Maybe I'll take classes while I'm a lady in waiting," she suggested.

"Good idea, baby," Simon told her, "but we're going to start house hunting soon so you'll be busy selecting furniture and instructing interior designers how you want to make our home."

"Can't wait," she said excitedly, "but how can you be so sure we're having a boy, Mama O?"

"Just intuition, Kim. I predicted all three of Marilena's children, even the twin boys," she said proudly.

~ * ~

In September 1996, Nell Flynn was home alone. Sean had gone to Sydney for a reunion of the hospitals' retired doctors. He would be away for a golfing weekend from Friday until Monday and Nell, strangely, relished the idea of having time to herself.

"Are you sure you don't mind, sweetheart?" Sean asked for the umpteenth time before he left.

"Of course I don't mind. I'll catch up on all the things I have been meaning to do for ages," she reassured him.

"Like what?" Sean was curious.

"Like cleaning out the laundry cupboards, sorting out my wardrobe..."

"Oh no! I'm not sure I like the sound of the latter. You will only be making room for new clothes. I can't keep up with you," Sean teased.

Nell ignored the remark. "I also thought I would meet up with Gina for a girls' lunch. I haven't seen her for a while," she continued, "But I'll miss you, darl. It isn't often we spend time apart these days."

"I'll miss you too, babe," he told her as he climbed into the taxi which would take him to the airport. "See you on Monday afternoon. I'll call!" And she watched as the taxi pulled out of the driveway and was soon out of sight at the bottom of the street.

Nell set about the laundry cupboards with enthusiasm. *Sean just dumps everything in here,* she thought as she tried to untangle lengths of cable and string. *I'll find a box for all his stuff and then at least I'll know where things are when he is frantically searching for something he knows he has, but can't find.* She smiled as she thought of him, the man who was her husband, lover, friend and soul mate. *Dear Sean—I love you so much and I'm not sure you understand the depth of my feelings,* she mused. *I am a completely different person now I'm with you; a new woman and God knows I needed to be...BUT...* She sighed deeply as she replaced the last bottle of fabric softener on the newly painted shelf... *I am going to do something this weekend I know I promised I wouldn't do, something I simply have to do. I know you won't understand or approve of my actions and nor will Joel, but I'm going to do it nonetheless.*

~ * ~

Joel's new job was keeping him very busy. "It seems like the whole population of WA has suddenly discovered they are entertainers," he told Sheralyn as they sat down for a rare dinner together.

"No work talk tonight, darl," she implored. "Let's just enjoy our time together as a family...well, I'd better qualify that. With Glenn living with Leanne now, and Helena spending most of her time with Dylan…" She paused as she pondered on what she had just said. "Do you think Helena will want to live with Dylan soon?"

"I hope not," Joel said pointedly. "She's isn't eighteen yet."

Sheralyn raised her eyebrows and looked directly at her husband. "Joel Winston," she admonished. "How can you say that? It's like the pan calling the kettle. She is eighteen in a couple of weeks and you left home at eighteen."

"Yes, but that was different, Sher. She hasn't got a mother trying to rule her every move and anyway, she's my daughter. I have to make sure she's all right." Joel directed his best and most loving smile towards his wife.

"Okay, daddy dearest," she said with a wink in his direction. "Now to get back to what I was saying…with Glenn being with Leanne and Helena hooked up with Dylan, we only have Jasmine here permanently now."

"I know, babe. Are we growing into boring old farts, do you think?" He grinned mischievously.

Sheralyn laughed. "You might be, but I'm not…"

Not what?" Jasmine asked as she joined them at the table.

"Do you think your parents are boring, Jas?" Joel asked the bright and bubbly teenager.

"W-e-l-l…" She paused dramatically and eyed them impishly. "You are the best mum and dad in the whole world. I have a mum who is a brilliant nurse, not to mention her prowess on the netball court, not bad for an oldie, and her fearless, adventurous approach to all the white knuckle rides at Dreamworld…"

"Hey, hold on a bit," Sheralyn interrupted. "You only got me on the Tower of Terror because your dad had gone fishing with Sean, and Nana went white just standing next to it!"

They all laughed at the thought of Nell almost throwing up at the mere idea of going on Wipeout. "Nan was green," Jasmine recalled, "and we had to delay lunch for half an hour until she recovered!"

"I can well imagine that," Joel said knowingly, "But what about your dad, princess?"

Jasmine put her elbows on the table and rested her chin in her hands. "Who else in my school can boast that their dad is a television star? Well, was. Actually I don't boast about it, otherwise I'd never get away with such blatant arrogance, but guess what," she challenged.

"What?" Joel asked not hiding the thrill he felt that his youngest child was proud of his achievements.

"I meant to tell you this before, but I forgot. A boy in my class told me some judge or other from England who was on *Performing for Australia* looks just like you, Dad," she announced proudly.

Joel looked at Sheralyn, who shrugged casually to hide her surprise. "Well, that's funny," he said nonchalantly.

"That's what I said. When the boy told me, I said, 'So what? She's very lucky then, isn't she?' He didn't say anything else 'cos the whole class knows I don't talk about you in school," Jasmine continued and enthusiastically tucked into her steak, chips and salad. "No more was said about it after that," she added with her mouth full of chips.

Joel silently counted his blessings and Sheralyn breathed a sigh of relief.

Later, as they lay in bed, Sheralyn snuggled up to him and whispered, "Are you okay, babe?"

Joel held her close. "Yes, I am. I was worried for a minute or two, but no harm done. Now the show isn't on air, there won't be any problems." His thoughts, however, weren't quite so clear. *I haven't told Sher about Gerry's phone call other than to say Robert and his new wife will be descending on us sometime in the next couple of months. Maybe I ought to have told her about Ben and Belinda, but I don't want to complicate things. I have to leave well alone. I just have to.*

~ * ~

Nell switched on the computer with some fear and trepidation. *I've watched Sean and Joel on these things, but I'm not sure I know what I'm doing even though Sean has shown me how to send e-mails and look things up on Google.* She waited patiently until all the little icons were in place on the screen, then she took the mouse in her right hand. Gently and cautiously she manoeuvered the little arrow until it hovered over the Google icon. Holding her breath, she rapidly double-clicked the left button as Sean had taught her. Her heart was thundering in her chest. *Why am I so scared?* she asked herself silently. *This is a machine, not a person. I'm seventy-three years old, damn it. I can use a mobile phone, switch on a television and even manage to record programmes, so why am I so afraid of pressing the wrong key on this thing?* She looked at the screen and delighted that she'd managed to find the Google home page. Deftly, her fingers skimmed the keyboard. *Thank goodness at least I learned how to type,* she thought with relief. She watched the search box as the words appeared. *Obertelli Theatrical Agency, Sydney.*

Twenty-two

Kimberley and Simon Obertelli moved into their new home exactly two weeks before Kim's due date. The past eight months had flown by and Simon worked at the agency as planned while Kim settled into her new life in Australia. "I heard from Melissa today," he told her when he arrived home from work on Friday evening.

"Oh good," Kim enthused. "How is she? Did she ask about me?"

"Sweetheart, it was just an e-mail, a work e-mail," Simon explained. "She has a street dance group she'd like to put into the exchange programme."

"And?" Kim asked. "Have we got anybody to send over there? We need to have potential acts on a waiting list."

Simon smiled and lovingly took hold of her hand. "Darl, we have it covered. I told you last week Tempo was ready to go asap. I know you have missed direct involvement with the exchange

166

programme, but we have to consider our baby as your priority at the moment. Not long now."

Almost as if on cue, Kim winced. "Ouch," she said with a grimace as she removed her hand from his. "That hurt, but it's gone now. Maybe a bit of wind."

"Are you sure?" Simon asked, concern etched all over his face.

"No, I'm not sure, but..." She winced again and this time the pain lasted longer. Clutching her belly, she sat on the cream leather couch that had been delivered only the day before. "I think maybe this is it, darling."

Simon sat bolt upright and grasped her hand again. "Do we need to go to the hospital? Shall I get your case? What shall I do, darl? Shall I call Mama?"

"Simon, calm down," she said laughing. "We don't have to do anything yet except time how long it is between the pains. Surely you remember what they taught us at ante-natal classes. I might not get another pain for an hour, maybe longer."

"But I want to help."

"And you will help just by being here so long as you don't fuss. You can get my case from the nursery if you like and put it by the front door ready for when we leave. It's been packed for the past couple of weeks," she instructed. "And Simon..."

He turned to face her as he was opening the door. "Yes?" he asked anxiously.

"Relax! Take a deep breath. Make a cup of tea. Anything to stop the panic!" she told him. "It's me who is having this baby."

He grinned. "I know, sweetheart, but I'm so excited."

It was two-thirty in the morning of Saturday, the twenty-first of September when Kim shook Simon and said, "Time to go, babe." Ten hours later, Jordan Benjamin Obertelli made his appearance in the world with a lusty cry to announce his arrival. His parents and grandparents were delighted...*Well, that's one set of happy grandparents at least,* Kim thought, as Mama O enthused about her new *nipote.*

"Benjamin?" Simon whispered as Kim held her baby close to her for the first time.

With tears in her eyes, she nodded slowly. "I like the name," she said poignantly and Simon nodded slowly in acceptance of her decision.

~ * ~

Nell studied the Obertelli Agency website with interest. She scanned the list and noted that Simon Obertelli was managing director. There were a number of administrative employees and several telephone numbers to contact the various departments. *Might as well go to the top,* she decided. *Simon Obertelli will surely have a contact number for Kimberley. I'll have to use all my powers of persuasion to convince him to pass it on.* Suddenly she sensed a feeling of guilt. It was fleeting, but nonetheless strong enough to make her reconsider her actions. *Nell,* she chastised herself. *You have waited for this moment for so long. Don't give up now. Call the number!*

"Obertelli Theatrical Agency. How can I help you?"

Nell took a deep breath. "Good morning. My name is Nell Flynn. I wonder if I might speak with Simon Obertelli, please."

The girl on the phone seemed quite dismissive. "Mr. Obertelli isn't here at the moment. Can I take a message?"

"I really would like to speak to him personally, if you don't mind," Nell told her.

"What are you calling about, ma'am?"

"It's a personal matter and not one that I am able to discuss with anybody else," Nell explained in friendly tones. "I'll leave my number, but I would like him to return the call in the next couple of days."

The girl clicked her tongue loudly. "I'm sorry, but I was speaking the truth when I said he is not in the office. He's on leave for the next four weeks, but I will tell him you called."

Nell was overcome with frustration. "Very well. It's probably best that I don't leave my number then. Thank you for your time. I'll call again in a month. Goodbye."

As she replaced the receiver, her sensible head took over. *Maybe I'm not meant to make contact with Kimberley after all, but I'll bide my time. No harm done for the time being and I won't have to inform Sean or Joel I made that call.*

~ * ~

Four weeks after his birth, Jordan Benjamin Obertelli was baptised at the church where Simon himself had been baptised. The Obertellis were delighted to welcome him into their family and friends from the entertainment world, including Ryan Fortune, the presenter on *Performing for Australia,* were invited to the reception back at the senior Obertelli house.

"Just look at him," Ryan said, admiring the beautiful baby in his mother's arms. "He has your lovely blonde hair and his eyes are turning brown now. No wonder about that since both you and Simon have brown eyes. I've only ever seen one other person with brown eyes and naturally blond hair; Joel Winston. He was very attractive in his younger days. I don't know what he's like now, but wow, was he popular with all the girls!"

Simon approached from behind Kim. "What's that you're saying, Ryan?"

Kim looked uncomfortable and Simon noticed. "Ryan was commenting on Jordan's blond hair and brown eyes," she said quietly.

"Oh I see. Figures I guess, with a mother like you, darl," Simon said quickly. "I think *nonna* would like to show off her newest grandchild to all her friends. Excuse us, Ryan. Please help yourself to refreshments."

"Will do," Ryan said, completely unaware that he had stirred the hornets' nest.

Simon and Kim discreetly went in to the study where they could be alone for a moment or two. "Are you all right, darling?" Simon asked as he kissed his wife on the cheek.

"Yes, I'm fine," she replied. "I'll have to get used to comments like that, I suppose. It seems my father has made quite an impression on the Australian public." She shrugged and smiled, an appreciative, affectionate and I love you smile at her husband.

"Come on," Simon said gently. "Let's get back before Mama sends out the posse to search for us."

Later that evening when they were back in their own home, they settled Jordan and snacked on smoked salmon and green salad while they listened to music. Kim was totally relaxed. "You know, I love smoked salmon and green salad. I'd never had it before I came to Australia, but there's something very more-ish about it. I'd like a glass of red wine, too, but I don't think my milk production would benefit from it. I'll stick with the spring water for now and hope Jordan can be weaned off the breast in a couple of months."

"You know best, Kim," Simon told her. "I'm looking forward to the time when I can feed him, but the timing has to be left in your capable hands. I just want what's best for our little boy."

"What's this CD?" Kim interrupted. "I like that voice. Makes a change from Jimmy Barnes and John Farnham."

Simon immediately listened more attentively to the background music and looked wide-eyed at Kim. "Oh my goodness," he exclaimed. "How on earth did that get in there?"

"What is it? And why are you so concerned?" she asked.

"Darl, it's Joel Winston's first album," Simon told her gently. "Dad and I were listening to some old tracks while you were in hospital. It must have got left in the music centre. Sorry, babe. I'll remove it."

"You'll do no such thing, Simon Obertelli," she scolded light-heartedly. "I like it and I need to know what everybody is raving on about when Joel Winston's name crops up. He's good, mind you, very good." She smiled and said appreciatively, "I feel quite proud of him in a strange, remote sort of way," and she winked impishly at her dumbfounded husband.

"What's all this about, Kim?" he asked.

"All what?" she said pointedly.

"Interest in Joel Winston all of a sudden," he stated equally as pointedly. "For over a year, you have avoided speaking about him even in conjunction with work. Why now?"

Kim looked at her husband with affection. "I see you with your parents and envy your closeness. I see your parents with Jordan and love the way they love him as part of their family," she said with a hint of regret in her tone.

Simon read her mood. "Let's call *your* parents," he coaxed gently.

"No!" she exclaimed. "I don't think I'm ready yet and I wouldn't know what to say."

"But the longer you leave it, the harder it's going to be to mend fences," Simon told her. "Are you really saying that you don't want them to know about Jordan? And anyway, where does Joel Winston fit in with all this? To be honest, he has never been a part of your family, has he?"

Kim sighed deeply. "No he hasn't, but I'm slowly coming to terms with the fact that he is my biological father. I thought about it a lot when I was pregnant. I kept trying to imagine my mother with Joel Winston, but I couldn't picture them together." She screwed up her nose, not in distaste, but in an effort to further imagine Joel and her mum. "Mum and Dad had always been the perfect couple for me as I was growing up. I never suspected a thing, but now I know what happened, I realise they aren't as perfect as I had thought them to be. It's a sobering thought."

Simon held her close. "Babe, don't torture yourself with something which is out of your control. It's good you're thinking more reasonably about it, though. It shows that time is healing the wounds a bit."

"That's true," she agreed. "I've even been considering contacting them sometime, but not yet. I'll deal with Joel Winston, too, when I am comfortable with it."

Twenty-three

When Jordan was six months old, Kimberley returned to work. Nonna O was only too willing to look after the baby two afternoons each week and a hired nanny cared for him on the other three. Working afternoons only, Kim was still able to be a hands-on mummy and that was important to her.

"Welcome back, darling," Simon greeted her on her first day. "Look what I've done for you," he said.

Kim directed her eyes to where Simon was pointing. "Oh, wonderful!" she enthused, "A desk by the window!"

"Yes, but please note, your chair faces inwards. I can't have you gazing through the window when you are supposed to be working," he joked.

"Yes sir, Mr. Obertelli, Sir!" Kim quipped and it wasn't long before she settled back into her old routine, albeit in Sydney and not in London.

Simon was going through his memos. *I wonder what this is,* he thought and then said to his wife, "There's an old message here from somebody called Nell Flynn."

"Could be a singer, or with a name like Flynn, an Irish dancer," Kim noted. "Call her back. We could be onto a winner. When names come out of the blue like that, it's often a lucky break. Irish singers have the best voices. Think about The Corrs and Sinead O'Connor."

"Ms. Flynn didn't leave her number, but she asked to speak to me personally." He grinned mischievously. "Maybe I've got a secret admirer," he quipped.

"Is that so? So long as she doesn't wear bright red lipstick and operate under the pseudonym Janine, it will be fine."

Simon laughed with her. "You know, having you in the office, if you'll pardon the expression, is great. I could even get you to make me a coffee when I feel like one."

"In your dreams, Obertelli," Kim retorted. "Equal partners in everything, so you can just as easily make coffee for me, but as far as the mysterious Nell Flynn is concerned, we'll just have to wait until she calls again. If she's ambitious and needs us, she'll call."

Both Kimberley and Simon had decided that weekends should be away from work and if artistes needed to be seen at weekends, they had trained reliable employees who would willingly work for double rates on Saturdays. Sunday was the traditional rest day for all concerned. On one particular Saturday evening, Kim made a startling announcement. "I'm going to contact Ben," she said. "He took the bull by the horns when he made his revelations." She paused to consider what came next. "I'm going to do it now. I hate to say this, but I guess I should really speak to my mother first, since she's the one who is my blood relative."

Simon looked at her questioningly. "Ben is the person you know as your father, Kim. Don't deny him that right after all this time. It's obvious you can't contact one without the other; they live together, so please include them both, darl. I don't want to tell you what to do, but it's just friendly advice."

"I know, sweetheart, and I have always been able to talk to him more easily than I could talk to Mum." She took a deep breath. "Let's do it."

Simon was shocked and it showed. "Now? This minute?" he asked. "Would you like me to leave you to it? I'll make a discreet exit while you talk."

"No, please don't leave. I need you to be here with me. My strength is in your love." She grinned. "That sounds a bit philosophical and dramatic, doesn't it?" she conceded, "But please stay." She looked at the clock. "Ten-fifteen here, so that will be…"

"Eleven-fifteen in the morning in the UK," Simon calculated. "Will they be at home at that time on a Saturday?"

"I don't know, but I'll soon find out."

~ * ~

When the telephone rang, Belinda had just returned from shopping and was still holding several bags of groceries. "Yes?" she asked sharply as she picked up the receiver.

"Mum?"

Belinda gasped. Adjusting the telephone so she might hear more clearly, she dropped the bags on the floor, scattering fruit and potatoes all over the hallway. "Kimberley? Is that you?" she asked tentatively.

"Yes." Kim was shaking inside, but she took a deep breath in order to maintain her composure. "I thought it was about time we broke the ice. Is Dad there?"

Now it was Belinda's turn to breathe deeply. "No, he isn't here at the moment," she said falteringly.

"Oh well, when will he be back?" Kim asked. "It really would be easier to talk to you both at the same time."

Belinda was quiet.

"Mum? Are you still there?" Kim enquired curiously.

"Yes, I'm here, but I don't know what to say," Belinda said with a hint of regret in her voice.

"What's wrong? Is this not the right time?" Kim asked, her tone becoming agitated.

"No, not really. But there'll never be a right time, Kim, so I might as well tell you straight out—your dad and I have split up," Belinda said coolly.

"You are joking," Kim exclaimed not hiding the astonishment she was feeling. "When did all this happen and why? Didn't either of you consider telling me before I asked?"

"You haven't been in touch, Kim, so how were we to know whether or not you would be interested in what was happening here?" Belinda told her, once again revealing the bitterness she had displayed on the day they chose to shatter Kim's world.

"Well, why have you split up?" Kim asked again as Simon's jaw dropped at the pronouncement.

"We don't love each other anymore," Belinda said curtly. "It's as simple as that. I'm living here in the house until we can sell it and your dad –Ben– is living in an apartment above the bank. It's easiest that way since we can't bear to be within sight of each other these days."

Kim felt the full onslaught of Belinda's resentment, but she silently resolved to keep calm and try to view the situation sensitively and sensibly. "I'm not sure I totally understand, but I'm sorry," she managed to say. "I have lots of news for you, too; for you both actually, but it might not be appropriate for me to tell you at the moment. I guess it will keep."

"Why not now?" Belinda asked. "Now is as good a time as any. Is it good news? And where are you calling from? Are you at Willow Bank, or Chelsea?"

Kim took another sharp intake of breath. "Neither," she revealed. "I'm in our home in Sydney. Simon and I were married two years ago. I sold up in London—Premier Plus and Willow Bank…"

"You did what?" Belinda exclaimed, the same old haughtiness appearing in her voice.

"Just stop, Mother," Kim demanded. "You can either listen, or put down the phone. I called to build a few bridges, but your attitude does nothing to inspire me. Now, do you want my news or not?" *She certainly knows how to press my buttons,* she thought.

"How would *I* know if I want your news?" she asked tersely, "And how can *you* be so self-righteous about your dad and me not telling you we'd split up when you have married and quit the country without so much as one word to us? That's so very typical of you, Kimberley," Belinda retaliated. *And so akin to Joel Winston as always,* she thought. "You are so like your father…" she continued acidly.

"Would that be Ben?" Kim asked with equal venom in her voice, "Or Joel?"

"Oh, claws in, Kimberley; dig in deep, won't you?" Belinda said. "Telling you the truth was the worst decision I ever made. Living with the deceit was much easier than this. If you hadn't high-tailed it to Australia in the first place, none of this would have happened. You would be none the wiser and Ben and I would still be together. This is all your fault, Kimberley, and I hope you are very happy."

"Why do you have to be such a bitch, Mother?" Kim said sadly. "I would never have believed I would say that to you of all people, but you certainly know how to bring out the worst in a person. No wonder Ben left you."

"And I love you too, Kimberley Mason…whoops, I mean Mrs. Obertelli," Belinda said sarcastically. "Now if you have finished, I'll say goodbye." *Why should I be concerned about her?* she thought. *She isn't bothered about me,* and she replaced the receiver without another word.

~ * ~

Kim flopped onto the settee and sobbed. Simon held her close, saying nothing until the tears subsided. "Are you going to be all right, baby?" he asked gently.

Kim dabbed away the tears and nodded. "Why has she suddenly become so bitter and twisted? I didn't ask to be born. I just happened on that fateful afternoon in Liverpool. I'm a child of the sixties and there must be a lot of us around. After all, that was the age of flower power and free love, wasn't it? If I can accept that, why can't my mother?"

"I don't know, babe, but you found the whole situation unbearable at first, didn't you?" he answered.

"True. I just needed to come to terms with it in my own way."

Simon gave her in a hug. "If it makes it any easier, I'm a child of that era too."

"Yes, but you were wanted, Si," she said. "Recent revelations tell me I couldn't possibly have been welcomed with open arms and it was the years of deceit that I found the hardest pill to swallow."

"I know, darl, but Ben wanted you. He also loved your mum and he *chose* to be your father. Surely that must mean something and I think you know that. Maybe when you have settled down, you can talk to him, too," Simon advised. "I can't imagine he'd be as bitter as your mum. I wish there was something I could do to ease your pain."

Kim took his hand and squeezed it gently. "You help just by being here and loving Jordan and me," she told him. "I do need to talk to Ben." She paused poignantly. "You know, I find it so difficult to refer to him as Dad at the moment, but I'll call him now. I'll have to call his mobile. I might as well get it all over with in one go."

~ * ~

"Hello? Ben Mason here."

"Hi," she said quietly.

"Kimberley?"

"Yes, it's me. Please don't be shocked," she pleaded and then she began to cry again.

"What is it, Princess?" Ben asked, with the usual tenderness she knew so well.

Kim took a deep breath and tried to explain. "I have just spoken to Mum. I wanted to mend fences, but she just threw my efforts back in my face. I had no idea you'd split up. I wish you'd told me, but then again…"

"No need to explain, sweetheart. I understand," Ben said gently. "Don't cry. It's so good to hear from you. How are you? Where are you? We need to talk, don't we?"

Kim relaxed at the sound of her father's voice, the gentle tone with which she had grown up, the fatherly understanding she had known all her life. "Where do we start?" she asked.

"We start right here and now," Ben told her. "No use going over old ground."

Kim sighed. "I really don't want to go down that road again," she said, "but there is so much to catch up. I'm in Sydney, Dad. This is my home now. I left London, Willow Bank and Premier Plus behind a couple of years ago."

"Did you, by gum?" Ben said with a hint of Lancashire humour returning in his tone.

"Simon and I married before we left the UK and we have a baby boy."

Ben caught his breath. "Congratulations to you both," he said. "Am I'm a grandpa then?"

"You are indeed, but you have to be Poppy here in Australia. Jordan is Australian born and will certainly speak the lingo when he begins to talk!" The atmosphere was pleasant and Kim was heartened by it.

"Jordan, eh? I like that," Ben said.

"And you'll like what I'm going to tell you now even more," she said with affection. "His name is Jordan Benjamin Obertelli."

There was a moment's silence as Kim heard Ben catch his breath at the other end of the line. "That means more to me than you will ever know, sweetheart. I'm not certain I deserve that acknowledgement, but I certainly appreciate it. Are you sure about giving him my name?"

"I'm very sure, Dad," Kim told him confidently. "It took me a long time to get my head round the circumstances of my birth, but I could never forget how great you have been as my dad. I love you; always did; always will."

Ben fought back his tears. "I love you too, princess."

"It's a pity Mum couldn't accept me in the same way," she said sadly. "She didn't even give me a chance to tell her about the baby. She actually blamed me for your separation."

Ben was aghast. "I don't believe it!" he exclaimed. "In all our married life, I have never known her to be so self-centred. She blames everybody but herself. I couldn't live with her and her self-righteous views any longer, Kim. She threw all her pent up hate and resentment at me in the end. The Belinda I loved for all those years disappeared. What is the point of being unhappy for the rest of my life? I'm so sorry it's had to end like this, but our divorce becomes absolute in a couple of weeks."

"Oh Dad, I'm sorry. I don't know what else to say."

"You've already said what I want to hear, sweetheart," Ben informed her. "Can we please be friends again? And when can I come to see my grandson?"

"Back to normal from this moment, Daddy," she said happily. "And you can come to visit anytime."

Twenty-four

"I'll have to do the trip to Tassie, babe," Simon told Kim at the end of another very busy week. "Jason and Kerry are going to Melbourne and the other two aren't ready to audition on their own yet. Do you mind holding the fort here till I get back? It'll only be a couple of days."

Kim sighed pretentiously. "You just want to be out of the office," she teased. "Is working with your wife too demanding?"

"Oh bugger! You caught me out," he joked. "This marriage lark is twenty-four seven and if I'd known that, I'd never have got on that plane to Singapore five years ago."

"It's not quite five years yet," Kim corrected him. "But when you consider what has happened in those four and a bit years, it seems to be much longer than that."

"The best years of my life," Simon said with affection. "But back to the necessities, do you mind running this place while I go interstate?"

"Of course I don't mind. It'll be quite like old times, but at the other end of the planet. I'll enjoy it, but I'll miss you, darling and so will Jordan."

"I'll be back in—what do you Brits say?" He paused and looked at his wife, who shrugged questioningly. "I'll be back in three shakes of a lamb's tail," he continued jovially.

He left the following morning, planning to return as soon as possible with the street dance crew he'd heard were taking Tasmania by storm.

~ * ~

When the telephone rang, Kim was taking a much-needed coffee break after a hectic morning in the office. "Call from the Gold Coast. Will you take it, Kim?"

"Gold Coast? Who is it?" she asked. "We don't have an office up there, do we?"

"No, but we often get calls from other agencies if they think we can accommodate their clients," the receptionist told her. "Shall I put her through?"

"Okay. It can't do any harm to see what she wants. Did you get her name?" Kim waited for a reply, but the call was put through before she received an answer.

"Kim Obertelli. How can I help you?"

The caller was silent for a moment.

"Hello? Can I help you?" Kim said again.

"Er... I was hoping to speak to Simon Obertelli," the caller revealed.

"Simon isn't in the office at the moment. I'm his wife and business partner. Can I help you?" *This is getting a bit tedious,* she thought.

"I am trying to contact Kimberley Mason, who was on *Performing for Australia* and I thought Mr. Obertelli might have her number in the UK," the caller continued.

Kim momentarily caught her breath, but felt no immediate need to give up her anonymity. "We don't give out private numbers, Ms...? Sorry I didn't catch your name."

"Flynn, Nell Flynn," she faltered.

Kim realised immediately the name was not new to her. "Oh, you called a while ago, didn't you? We wondered why you didn't leave your number. If you would like us to represent you, you'll have to have an audition. Do you sing?" Then she heard a long, loud sigh coming from Nell.

"You have absolutely no idea who I am, have you?" Nell stated slowly and deliberately.

"Should I?" Kim asked curiously.

"I *am* correct in assuming you are the Kimberley Mason I am trying to contact," Nell ventured.

Kim was concerned. "Why would you assume that?" she asked cautiously.

"Your Bolton accent is a dead give-away, in spite of your Italian name."

Kim had to smile. "I might also say that your Scouse accent also tells me that *you're* not as Irish as your name suggests, either."

Nell felt herself becoming irritated. The old Nell was rearing its ugly head and she needed to keep her emotions under control. "I'm not Scouse as you put it," she said haughtily, "but I do come from the Liverpool area originally."

"Ms. Flynn," Kim said pointedly. "Is there a specific reason for this call? The Obertelli Agency is very busy and I really don't have time for a social chat."

"You are certainly your father's child," Nell said pointedly.

Kim was shocked. "What on earth do you mean?" she asked, deliberately trying to stay calm. "I have to say there is something in your manner I don't like and might be construed as offensive."

Nell breathed deeply. "I apologise, sincerely. Please forgive me. I have no intentions of upsetting you. Actually, I feel quite nervous about speaking to you."

"If I might be so bold, you are making me nervous, too," Kim told her. "What is it you want, Ms. Flynn?"

Nell was blunt. "I'm Joel Winston's mother."

"Excuse me?" Kim asked with measured calm.

"I'm Joel Winston's mother," Nell repeated, "and that makes me..."

"If it's Joel Winston you want, you have called the wrong office," Kim said, deliberately keeping her emotions under control. "I'll get my secretary to give you the number of the Perth office..." She swiftly returned to the switchboard. "Jill, please give Mrs. Flynn the number of the Perth office." And then, "Goodbye, Mrs. Flynn." Kim replaced the receiver and suddenly began to shake uncontrollably.

~ * ~

When Simon returned, Kim gave him the details of the call. "She recognised me from my accent," she explained, "but I didn't acknowledge who I was."

"What harm would it have done to admit who you are, Kim?" Simon asked gently. "You have done nothing to be ashamed of. And anyway, as his mother, she would have had his number, wouldn't she? Not the best way out, Kim, was it?"

"I wasn't thinking straight. The woman got under my skin straight away. She sounded so supercilious," she told him. "If she's my grandmother, I'm not sure I want to acknowledge the fact. Apart from that, how would she know I have been told about my parentage? Even Joel Winston has never acknowledged our link in spite of his working in the Perth office. Dad said Joel respected their demands to have nothing to do with me. Nell Flynn has broken a promise that was made thirty odd years ago. The audacity of her!"

Simon grinned. "Don't hate me for saying this, babe, but the superciliousness sure does sound like a family trait! Listen to yourself."

Kim recognised the truth in his comment. "Yeah, I guess so," she conceded. "Oh dear, maybe I am my father's daughter after all!"

They both laughed; Kim guardedly. *Talk about the sins of the father; will I ever really be able to come to terms with who I am?*

Twenty-five

The whole world was abuzz with plans for the new millennium. Whilst New Zealand would see in the year 2000 before Australia, preparations in Sydney were lavish and typically impressive.

In December 1999, Kim could hardly contain her excitement. "I can't wait to see Dad and his new lady friend," she told the Obertellis over Sunday lunch a week before Christmas. "We have so much ground to catch up and he sounded so happy when I spoke to him. Jenny must be good for him. Tony and Liz are joining us, too, on the twenty-eighth, so it will be a wonderful reunion and not before time."

Mama O smiled at her daughter-in-law. "We are all so pleased you and your family are on good terms again. Whatever it was that caused the problem must now be over, even though it was such a sad event that began to heal the wound. Good luck, Kimberley. You deserve it."

"Thank you, Mama O," she replied. "I have found it very difficult to talk openly about it, but things have improved recently after the past few traumatic years." *If only you knew the real truth, Mama O,* she thought sadly, *but the whole story is far too complicated to reveal.* "And yes, my mother's death really shocked us all. We have to assume the brain tumour may be blamed for much of the heartache she caused leading up to her sudden death. I don't think I'll ever totally get over it. She didn't go to see a doctor until it was too late. She just seemed to grow angrier and angrier with everybody. Personally, I have to believe she didn't know what she was doing." Tears welled up in sad eyes. "She and I never sorted out our differences and that's so sad."

"And what about your papa?"

Kim shrugged. "Who knows what he must have felt when he found out Mum was so sick," Kim said. "They had been divorced for only a few months. He moved back in with her to look after her, but she passed away very quickly. Poor man. He had loved her for so long and then all of a sudden her life was snuffed out like a candle. We don't know what's waiting round the corner, do we?"

Simon reached out across the table and took Kim's hand. "Don't cry, darling," he said. We can't dwell on these things. Remember the good times. I'm sure that's what Ben is doing."

"Sorry," she said. "I'm okay really. It's just that I never got to say goodbye and it gets to me occasionally. Christmas time has an odd way of bringing out our regrets and insecurities."

"Do you pray, Kim?" Shane Obertelli asked.

"Not really," she replied. "But I do see the value of prayer sometimes."

"We'll pray for you, Mama O and I," he said gently. "But remember, life is for the living. We never understand the reasons why people die before their time."

"I know that and I also know the mother I last spoke to was not the mother I had known for most of my life. Thank you, Papa" she said. "I appreciate your kind words. The new millennium will be a brand new start for us all."

~ * ~

Ben arrived in Sydney with Jenny on December twenty-third. Kim had paced up and down the airport arrivals hall for an hour before the plane was due to land.

"Keep still, Mummy," the four year old Jordan said. "Sit here with Daddy and me. Poppy Ben will be here soon."

"I know, sweetheart," she told the little boy who wriggled about, trying to contain his own excitement at meeting his other pop, and then Ben appeared pushing a trolley laden with several suitcases, the broadest and happiest of smiles on his face.

Kim ran to meet him and threw her arms around him. "Welcome to Australia, Dad!" she cried. "It's oh so good to see you."

When they could bear to separate, Ben introduced Jenny. "This is Jenny," he said lifting her left hand to display a shiny new wedding ring.

"Hi, Jenny!" Kim said, "And congratulations!" She looked at her dad. "You could have told us," she scolded, "but then…"

"We wanted it to be a surprise," Ben told them. "And anyway…"

"Okay, okay," Kim conceded. "I can't complain, can I, but please don't present me with a new sibling as well," she joked, thinking that she and Simon had presented him with a grandson when she divulged to her father the news of her own marriage.

"Well, now that you mention it…" Ben added impishly.

Jenny laughed. "I don't think so," she said, "unless it's by divine intervention. My body clock has told me it's time to stop thinking about babies. I have two grown-up children from my first marriage. Only grandchildren from now on for us."

"Phew!" Kim exclaimed. "I don't think I could cope with a brother or sister younger than its uncle."

"What do you mean, Mummy?" Jordan asked, moving forward to meet his poppy for the first time.

Ben scooped him up into his arms. "She's just being silly, young man and hello, my big boy. Am I pleased to see you!"

Jordan hugged him tightly. "Have you brought your swimmers, Poppy?" he asked. "I can swim with my armbands on and I need you to come in my pool with me when we get home."

"No jetlag allowed," Simon quipped. "Welcome to Sydney, Ben. Good to see you."

~ * ~

Shane Obertelli had big plans for welcoming in the year 2000. "We'll gather all our family together in the park on the north side of the bridge near Kirribilli," he announced. "If we go early enough, we'll get a prime position. Take Jordan's sleeping bag and he can sleep when he feels like it. Lui's kids are old enough now to stay awake."

"Do we have any say in this, Papa?" Simon asked. "You seem to have it all organised in typical Obertelli take-over style."

"You just get your butts up there in good time. The wait will be long, but we can keep the children occupied and have a picnic dinner. There'll be live music in the park. We have to show the Masons how Australians celebrate."

Twenty-six

"We just have to be together for this special New Year," Nell told Joel in the lead up to Christmas.

"I'm working right up to Christmas Eve, Mum," Joel told her. "The kids are all home again for Christmas Day and…"

"I have an idea," Nell interrupted. "We'll all meet in Sydney and see the new millennium in by the Harbour Bridge. Sean's ex-colleague is going to London and has offered us his house for the Christmas period if we want it. It's too good an opportunity to miss. It's a massive house near Kirribilli so Glenn and Helena can bring their partners if they would like to come and join us for a family celebration. What do you think?"

Joel sighed. "You'll never change, will you, Mother?"

"Don't you dare call me Mother. You know how much I hate it. Makes me sound old and matriarchal."

Joel had to smile as he recalled again his run-in with Nell that caused him to leave home, but he'd gone over his past so often recently that he decided instantly not to go down that road again. *The year 2000 will be a brand new start for us all.*

"Look," he said, gathering his thoughts in the present again, "I'll discuss it with Sheralyn and the kids and let you know later."

~ * ~

The Obertelli family and friends gathered early on New Year's Eve. "Shane never does anything simply," Mama O explained to Ben and Jenny as they put up trestle tables and made sure there were enough chairs for everybody. "This picnic will be nothing short of a banquet."

"Looks excellent to me," Ben said. "I can well understand why Kim adapted so quickly to this lifestyle. I can see Tony and Liz wanting to migrate, too, after this."

"Would that be so bad?" Mama O asked.

"Well, no not really. I would want to see my children settled. I would never stand in the way of their ambitions, but I would miss them terribly."

"I'm sure you would, but you might decide to join them here, too," she suggested.

"I think I might look into it," Ben said, but he was interrupted by a very excited little boy.

"Come on, Poppy Ben," Jordan cried. "I need to show you something."

"Everything is always needed urgently," his *nonna* commented.

"I've noticed," Ben said laughing and to his grandson, "But I'm helping *Nonna* with the chairs."

"You go, Ben, but be back by seven thirty. We'll eat while the entertainment is on. Shane says it will be spectacular. Jenny and I will put the world to rights while you're away," the Italian matriarch said. "The bambino comes first."

"I'm not a *bambino, Nonna,*" the little boy complained. "I'm four!" He took hold of Ben's hand to lead him to his favourite place in the park.

As they prepared to leave, Shane appeared, his face lit with excitement. "Look who's here," he called pointing in the direction of the park entrance.

Every member of the group turned strained eyes towards the gates. Mama O was the first to shriek out loudly. "Bianca! My Bianca!" she cried and she ran to her daughter whom she hadn't seen for more than five years. "Shane Obertelli," she called. "I'll deal with you later!" She swept up her daughter in her arms and smothered her with kisses. "You naughty girl," she scolded. "Why didn't you tell me you were in Australia? We only spoke last night; you naughty, naughty girl."

"And spoil the surprise?" Shane called out. *Secrets and Mama O do not go well together,* he thought. *Wait until later when they find out what my next surprise is.* He chuckled to himself, knowing he had the ace up his sleeve.

Jordan was impatient. "Come on, Poppy," he urged. "We can see Auntie 'anca after we've been to see the swans."

"Excuse us, please," Ben said with a wink in the direction of his daughter and soon he and his grandson stood on the banks of the lake in the evening sunshine and watched the black swans gliding gracefully across the clear blue waters. *Idyllic,* Ben thought with a happy sigh, *just perfect.*

~ * ~

"I'm going for a stroll," Joel told his family. "Is anybody coming? I promise I won't be long."

No response was forthcoming from the bodies relaxing on sun loungers. They were taking the evening sun after gorging themselves on a picnic of seafood and salad, gateau and ice cream.

"I'll take that as a no then," he conceded and set off in the direction of the lake.

~ * ~

The setting sun provided an incongruous glare on an otherwise perfect vista. Ben reflected later that it had given the lake an enigmatic air, the ominous forecasting of an event that in his wildest dreams he would never have envisioned. He had shielded his eyes against the brightness.

"What the…?" He stood stock-still not knowing what he should do. *Do I turn and head back to the family without acknowledging him? Do I really want to see him? Do I pretend I haven't seen him and say nothing, not even to Kim?* His thoughts were those of schoolboy panic and he hated himself for it. He took a deep breath. *Ben Mason,* he chastised himself, *you are a grown man. You have no axe to grind anymore. This is what Belinda dreaded would happen to Kim and now it has happened, not to Kim, but to you. Handle it.* But his positive thoughts did not prevent his heart from beating wildly in his chest.

~ * ~

Joel was lost in thought as he wandered away from his family. *This is one mighty big secret I have kept from them. I'm not sure they'll ever forgive me…well, Sheralyn will, but my mother will make sure I suffer for the next few months. I still don't know how I'll deal with the Obertellis. Shane said this was his surprise—to have me perform for the very last time. He didn't want anybody to know except the two of us. Typical, flamboyant Shane. He obviously doesn't know of my connection with Kimberley and I have to question my own wisdom in agreeing to this madcap scheme.* He stopped to watch a little boy running along the banks of the lake towards several bigger boys who were fishing, the child excitedly calling out, "Come on, Poppy Ben!"

For the two men, it was as if time stood still and everything was happening in slow motion. Within seconds, though, they were rushing forward to greet each other and shaking hands, very formally at first, but then with all caution thrown to the wind, they were hugging away the long years the best mates had been apart.

"What the hell are you doing here?" Joel asked.

"Could say the same to you, Joel," Ben replied. "This certainly wasn't on my holiday agenda."

They looked at each other questioningly and neither saw the answer in the other's expression.

"Can we talk?" Joel asked sheepishly.

"We have to," Ben replied, "if we are to live this down with our respective families."

"How long have we got?" Joel asked. "We've eaten, but I have an appointment to keep at seven thirty."

"That's when we are eating, so we have..." He paused to look at his watch. "...forty five minutes. But I must keep my eye on the little boy over there watching the guys fishing. He's my grandson, Jordan Obertelli."

Joel smiled as they sat down on the grass, making sure they kept an eye on that little boy. "I heard about him on the grapevine. We can't all work for the same organisation without hearing what's going on within the establishment, but..."

Ben put his hand on Joel's shoulder. "I know, mate. Don't worry. I also know you have never broken your promise and I appreciate that very much."

Joel nodded slowly. "Gerry told me about your split with Belinda and I wanted to talk to you then, but he advised me to leave well enough alone. It's been difficult, especially since Kim was on TV. It took three of us to stop my mother from contacting her. You know what my mother's like, but..."

Ben grinned. "Yes I do and sorry Joel, but she did contact Kim at the office soon after she'd had Jordan."

"What?" Joel gasped, exasperated. "She never told us; typical of her. Just wait until I see her."

"Kim had her wits about her and didn't acknowledge her, not because of any animosity, but because she didn't know how to handle it," Ben explained. "No harm done on that score."

"My mother probably didn't like to admit she had been rebuffed. Good on Kim, I say. It would have put Nell Flynn in her place and not many people can do that!"

Ben looked out across the lake, before he said quietly, "You heard about Belinda's death, didn't you?"

Joel looked embarrassed. "Yes, I did and I am so sorry. I ought to have written to you, at least, I could have sent a sympathy card, but I felt so guilty that I might have been at the root of all her problems and I'd be the last person you would want to hear from. How does one deal with that, Ben? I mean, I'm not feeling sorry for myself, but the fact that I..." He couldn't continue, because the lump in his throat was threatening to choke him.

Ben placed his arm across Joel's shoulders again to reassure him. "I forgave you long ago, you know that. Your honesty from the start really paved the way for me to marry Belinda. I knew she didn't love me, but I was prepared to work on it and for a long time, it did work. I thought Belinda had come to terms with it all, but something wouldn't let her accept that those things happen sometimes. Our biggest mistake was keeping it a secret from Kim. When we told her, she was devastated, but thankfully, time has healed the wounds. She's an intelligent girl, bright, witty and very down to earth." He paused deliberately. "She's a very worldly person and she has a lot of you AND me in her," he said laughing. "I can live with that now."

Joel didn't hide his astonishment. "Well, Ben Mason," he conceded, "I never thought I'd hear you say that, but if you can live with it, so can I."

"Mates again?" Ben asked smiling at his childhood friend.

Joel breathed in deeply to keep control of his emotions. "Mates," he said, "Bloody good mates."

As if on cue, Jordan came running up to them. "Is it dinner time yet, Pop? I'm starving."

"It is indeed time for dinner, so we'd better be getting back," Ben told the little boy. "This is a friend of mine from way, way back in England. We were your age when we met. Now isn't that a long time ago?"

Jordan looked bemused. "I didn't know you used to be four," he said matter-of-factly.

The two men laughed and shook hands again. "Maybe I'll see you later," Joel told him. "You'll never guess what Shane is pulling out of the bag."

Ben looked squarely at Joel. "I think I might guess, now that I've seen you," he said. "Does he know exactly what he's doing?"

Joel shrugged. "We'll deal with it, won't we?" he asked cautiously. "But what about...?

Ben smiled. "Kim? She'll be fine, I know it and yes, we will deal with it. See you then."

Twenty-seven

"How confident are you feeling?" Ben asked Kim as he manipulated a brief moment away from the rest of the family.

"What do you mean?" she asked curiously.

Ben took her hands in his and looked into her eyes, eyes that were sparkling with happiness, eyes that told him what he wanted to know.

"I'm good, Dad. Hit me with whatever you've got."

"Shane has a massive surprise for everybody. I won't tell you what it is as it will steal his thunder. I just need to know that you can handle the surprise," Ben told her.

"Is it good?" she asked with some trepidation. "You are freaking me out now."

"I think it could be, but then I know what it is," he continued, "We are nearly in the year two thousand and the whole world must be viewed through understanding eyes, but look, it's starting

and we'd better take our seats at the table. It's all good, Princess."
Please God.

At seven-thirty precisely, the lights went up on the temporary stage that had been erected earlier in the day. Shane walked on stage and was seen all around the park on enormous TV screens strategically placed to allow everybody to enjoy the show.

~ * ~

Kim watched the dancers, the singers and the comedy acts through knowledgeable eyes. *Shane hasn't lost his touch,* she thought as she smiled across at her husband. Simon nodded in appreciation and then Shane appeared again to introduce the final act.

"Ladies and gentlemen, boys and girls," he began. "The next act is my millennium treat for you all. In my opinion, he has been one of the most successful artistes ever to grace the shores of Australia. Children loved him, teenagers adored him, parents admired him."

Kim automatically took hold of her father's hand and held on tight.

Shane continued. "...And now for one last time, he has agreed to perform for you."

An expectant hush went around the park. "Ladies and gentlemen, please give a grand old Sydney welcome to..." When Joel walked on stage, the place erupted; ecstatic cheers, adoring screams, happy tears for their idol of yesteryear.

~ * ~

"This is something I have to do by myself," she told Simon when the performance was over. "Please sidetrack your papa. I would like to speak to Joel Winston alone."

Ben placed his hands on her shoulders and looked directly into her eyes again, eyes that were shining with admiration for the man in front of her. "Are you sure, Kim?"

She nodded and made her way backstage with Simon, who was to take his father away from something that had the potential to become a situation completely overtaken by emotion. Kim waited discreetly until Simon walked off with his father. Joel had his back to her and was busy freshening up, oblivious of what was going on around him.

"You're still pretty good," she said quietly.

Joel turned to face her. "Hi," he said calmly. "How are you?"

"I'm good and you?"

He nodded. "Thanks for the compliment, but my days of performing are over. I know when it's time to go."

Kim smiled and nodded slowly. "My dad will be pacing the floor now, wondering what is going on," she told him.

"I can well imagine," Joel agreed, "but he has nothing to fear."

"You and I both know that, but I needed to speak to you—correction—I *wanted* to speak to you. I had no idea my opportunity would come so unexpectedly and I have not prepared myself for this meeting."

Joel motioned to her to take a seat. "Nor I, but after tonight, it's unlikely I'll be in Sydney again for a very long time, if ever. As far as I'm concerned, a promise is a promise."

"Does your mother know that?" Kim asked gently and without animosity.

"She should, and as soon as I've finished here, she will be reminded of such," he assured Kim. "Please accept my apologies. I had no idea she had broken our promise until I bumped into your dad earlier."

"Dad has always spoken highly of you in spite of..."

"What I did?" Joel interrupted.

Kim smiled again. "Look, Joel...you don't mind if I call you Joel?"

"Not at all. That's my name," he said with the mischievous grin Kim had noticed in the picture on the sleeve of his first album. "So long as you don't tell me it's posh."

Kim looked at him questioningly.

"Long story,' he said.

Kim took a deep breath. "I bear you no malice," she told him. "After all, I wouldn't be standing here but for you. I am worldly-wise enough to know these things happen, unlike my mother who took to her grave her dislike of what you did. I don't agree with her views. I hated you for a while for not acknowledging me, but in a strange kind of way, I admire you and I'm quite proud of your success. I have clearly benefitted from your talent. It must be in the genes."

"Thanks for that," Joel said, "but you really don't need to justify what I did. I'm not proud of what happened in the Connollys' attic room thirty odd years ago."

"Ah, Uncle Gerry and Auntie Penny," she recalled with a smile. "I was angry with them, too, for a while, but who could be mad at them for long? I love them to bits, even if Uncle Gerry does support Liverpool!" She paused and then laughed cordially. "Look at us two," she continued. "It's almost like looking in a mirror."

"I know," he agreed.

"And it's been noticed, but we have never informed Shane of my pedigree and he's been tactful enough not to cast aspersions."

Joel nodded slowly again. "He'll hear nothing from me."

"I trust you," Kim told him. She paused and then took a deep breath. "What I am going to say now, is said first and foremost out of respect and admiration for my dad and also for you in an odd kind of way. Ben is my dad; always has been and always will be. He has been the best dad I could have wished for and also the nicest, sweetest and most caring person in the whole world."

"I totally agree with you, Kim. Ben was my best friend from being four years old. I let him down big time, but he forgave me. Keeping his promise was easy, because I did it out of love and friendship. Earlier when we met, it was as if time stood still and we were miraculously able to reclaim the trust and admiration we held for each other all those years ago. That's what I call true friendship." He stopped as the lump in his throat prevented him from speaking further.

Kim noticed and took his hand in hers. "Joel," she said gently. "I have a wonderful family." He nodded in agreement. "And I don't want another. I trust you will understand that this will be our only conversation on the matter. I bear you no hard feelings; in fact I really do like you."

Joel regained his composure. "Thank you, Kim," he said. "I understand. Both our families have their own lives to lead without disruptions in what we all know as happy family lives." He squeezed her hand gently. "And I really like you, too."

Kim sighed with relief. "That was easier than I thought it would be. Thank you and I think I might now be able to take your calls in the office. Business as usual!" she quipped.

"That's my girl!" he answered without thinking and then looked mortified at what he had just said.

Kim nudged him playfully. "In your dreams," she said and they laughed together.

~ * ~

Joel soon returned to his family after his surprise performance. "How did I do?" he asked.

Sheralyn gave him a caring hug. "It was an appropriate swansong and an ideal start to a brand new year, darl," she said with affection. The kids agreed enthusiastically.

Nell looked at him sternly. "Keeping secrets from your family, Joel Winston, is not good. Not only that, you said you were going for a walk and didn't return for three hours. You promised not to be long."

"Don't start, Mother," he said quietly but firmly as he sat down beside her. "*You* have no need to reprimand *me* as far as keeping promises is concerned." He looked her squarely in the eye. "Now, regarding Kimberley..."

Meet Vera Berry Burrows

Vera Berry Burrows is a UK-born former teacher of English Language and Literature, living in Queensland, Australia with journalist husband, Alan. She has a son and two grandsons living in the UK. She has been writing for a number of years and has had numerous non-fiction articles published in the UK and in Australia. She was educated at Farnworth Grammar School in Lancashire, trained as a teacher at St Katharine's College, Liverpool and gained a Bachelor of Arts degree with the Open University.

Since she took early retirement in 1994 having been in the teaching profession for thirty-one years, writing has become her compulsive hobby. *Regarding Kimberley* is her second published novel.

Works by Vera Berry Burrows

Tomorrow Never Comes - Marriage, a new home and a new baby, Joel Thomas, all make up a perfect life for Nell Winston until suddenly her husband is no longer there and she turns into a woman possessed of compulsion to rule her son. Her strength is drawn from her unwavering sense to control until the young Joel decides to make a stand against her. Her domineering, self-absorption, along with egotistical stubbornness, takes her into a life that becomes her worst nightmare.

Joel's apparently selfish show of independence leads him along an extremely rocky road to eventual success in the Swinging 60's and with a complete reversal of roles, he takes charge of his mother's life. Will the new start in a different country bring the fulfillment they are both seeking?

Regarding Kimberley - Show business executive Kimberley Mason always felt something was missing from her life. She forms an association with a theatrical agency in Australia and uncovers a secret kept by her parents for thirty years. Revelations about her birth shatter her world. Discovering her real father is Australian television celebrity Joel Winston, she cuts herself off from the family she had always thought to be perfect

Leaving behind her past in England, she moves to Australia to be with the man she loves, her business partner, Simon Obertelli. Will running away ensure her future happiness or will the complications of accepting her famous father only lead to heartache?

Connections - Jane O'Connell did not envisage that her early retirement would completely disrupt her life. With too much time on her hands, she finds it difficult to adjust to her new existence. In her obstinate selfishness, she alienates herself from her family and friends. Running away from all things familiar appears to be her only option, but is it? Will the connections she makes really solve the problems she encounters in her life after work?

Family Matters - For three children left without a mother in the middle of World War Two, survival was all they could hope for. Their father struggled as a single parent, but instilled into his children, determination, ambition and self-respect so that they might succeed in post-war years and achieve everything which he was denied during his life.

This is their story.

My Name is Aphrodite - Rodi Bartlett sits on a plane taking her to the land of her conception. She can't call it the land of her birth because when her mother was sixteen years old, she had flown back to England from Corfu at the end of two weeks in the sun, unaware she was pregnant. When her mother, Adele dies young, details of the father, Cory Demetriou are exposed in her will and he has never been told of his daughter's existence.

Rodi's relentless search for the father she has never known, takes her to Corfu, mainland Greece and beyond. Filled with determination, setbacks, hope and love, this is the story of a young woman's quest to fulfil her mother's dying wish, but will Cory Demetriou accept her as his daughter twenty-six years on?

Dare To Dream - Left on the doorstep of St Anthony's Catholic Orphanage in Bolton, Northern England, Anne Marie O'Shea is placed in the guiding hands of another orphan named Bella Jones. As the years pass by, Bella accepts her lot for what it is; Annie dreams of a wonderful life, that special bit of magic that everybody deserves. When Bella is killed in a road accident at the age of twenty, Annie is left to fend for herself, to make decisions about her future and combat all the fears she has about forming lasting relationships. With numerous ups and downs, nurse training and emigration to Australia, a series of unbelievable co-incidences eventually puts the magic in her life that she could previously only dream about.

Payback - Julietta's holiday becomes a nightmare when she is swept up in the frenzy of other people's abhorrent need for revenge.

VISIT OUR WEBSITE

FOR THE FULL INVENTORY
OF QUALITY BOOKS:

http://www.wings-press.com

Quality trade paperbacks and downloads
in multiple formats,
in genres ranging from light romantic comedy to
general fiction and horror. Wings has something
for every reader's taste.
Visit the website, then bookmark it.
We add new titles each month!